Ripples on the Lake

Ripples on the Lake

Mel O'Dea

First edition published as *Driftwood Memories* in 2015 by Arena Books
Second Edition published as *Ripples on the Lake* in 2024 by The Forest Press

www.theforestpress.co.uk

Mel O'Dea
Ripples on the Lake

British Library cataloguing in Publication Data. A catalogue record for this
Book is available from the British Library.

Thema categories: FBA; FXB; FXM; FXL; FXN; FXD; 1DDR; 1DDU-GB-ESL;
3MPQX; 3MPQZ; FBAN; DC.

Cover design by Becca Thorne

ISBN: 978-1-0687964-1-8 Print
ISBN: 978-1-0687964-0-1 eBook

Printed and bound in Great Britain by Clays Ltd, Elcograf S.p.A.

For all those who walked with me along life's rocky path.

1

In prison one has time, so I thought I would write it all down. Maybe seeking some sort of therapy, I don't know.

I first met Mary when I was 16. She was in our garden, pulling weeds, her shock of red hair catching shards of sunlight. I watched her move, she moved with a quiet deliberation, bending down, pulling the weeds, straightening up again. Her movements rhythmical in their purpose. She stopped for a moment and lit up a cigarette. So, she smokes. So do I. A point of contact?

For the next week I watched her through the window, watching her hair sparkle in the sun, moving with every movement. Then I decided that I would go out and speak to her ...

Sorry to bother you, but have you got a cigarette?

She looked at me. *Sure*

What's your name?

Mary. And yours?

John. Would you like to go for a walk sometime?

Sure.

Tomorrow? After lunch? Around 3?

Sure, I'll meet you here at 3 …

Strange exhilaration. I feel shy and yet excited …

3pm. I leave the house claiming to my parents that I'm taking the dogs out. They look at me silently exuding disinterest. Father picks up the paper again and Mother continues with the washing up. She rubs the plates compulsively with an old cloth and says nothing. It was always this way with Mother and Father. They did not say much. And each had their routine. Father's routine was the *Irish Times* and Mother's the washing up. They existed within their own peculiar rituals, seeking comfort in hiding behind their routines so that they weren't forced to communicate with each other. Father would read the paper and then go into the television room, silently watching the television whilst drinking glass after glass of whiskey before finally falling asleep in his chair. Mother would wash up and cook. She existed in her own oblivion, peeling the potatoes with subliminal aggression and performing her tasks with a fixated compulsion that I would never understand. Repeated movements. Each repetition finding its own fruition.

We hide ourselves like this. We cut off from life. The birds sing outside and the sun breaks through the window but none of this is acknowledged. Just the repetition of movements, the search for a silence that gives us an excuse not to be …

I didn't know if Mary would turn up. It seemed too much to hope for. But she was there, her face smiling in the sun, her hair glistening. I ask her whether she would like to walk to the lake, *It is one of my favorite places. I go there when I'm fed up.*

Sure.

So we walk. At first we walk in silence, looking at each other but not saying anything. Then I ask, *Where do you live?*

In the village. The cottage on the hill beside the church.

What's it like?

It's ok. My father works as the postman and my mother looks after the house and my five brothers. I work here to get a bit of money. But really I want to go to college. Somewhere far from here. Maybe in the United Kingdom. Escape from the curtain twitching here. Your business is everybody's business. I go to school at the convent. Don't like it much. The nuns are strict.

And I don't find the lessons interesting. But I go. Even if I just spend the whole class staring out the window. I watch the birds. I like to connect with their freedom. The teacher yells at me to pay attention. For a while I feign interest in declining Irish verbs. Then I start looking out the window again. I play with the sunlight, catching it and embracing it with my hands. Fingering it as if it was some sort of ephemeral liquid that pours through my fingers. My parents call me a dreamer. But that's okay. I think they feel that I'm not 'normal' in the way they think is 'normal'. In a funny way, I see that as a compliment. Out of my five brothers, two work and three are in school. They're younger than me. My parents favour them. I think that they feel that boys ultimately have more potential. So I'm expected to help out at home, with the cooking, the cleaning. My brothers watch TV. My parents encourage the three that are in school with their studies. They say that there's no real point in me going to college because I'll only end up getting married anyway. One of the brothers who works is a plumber. The other is an electrician. My parents are proud of them. They don't have to do anything in the house. When they come in from work, I have to make them each a mug of tea. Never really understood why they can't make it themselves. It's easy to boil a kettle and throw a teabag into a mug. But there you go. So, I go to school, watch the birds, come home, clean the house, help with the dinner, and then go to bed. I dream of more. I dream of seeing the world. When I mop the kitchen floor I retreat into those dreams. I have a postcard of an island in the Caribbean. When I feel caught, I look at it. The sun glinting on the pure white sand. The azure sparkle of the sea. The coconut palms waving in the breeze. I imagine I am there, traveling in my mind and dipping my feet into the azure, watching the flick flick of fishes upon the reef, embracing myself with their color. And no one else is there. Just me and my dreaming. I bring the postcard to school and look at it. The maths teacher writes equations on the blackboard. But I am not there at all. I am on the small island. I am floating through the sky and feeling the clouds pass through my fingers. The sun warms my face and wraps itself around me like a healing blanket, like the ultimate escape. I am Houdini. I can escape any time I want. I float outside the classroom window. I move through the air and with the possibilities that make up my life. I see each potential, and move through it. I exist above it all. Giant steps are what one takes whilst walking on the moon ...

I smile at her. Her radiance catches me. She seems to sing the songline of ages, something primitive, something complicated at the same time. I watch her walk. Her feet on the grass and tiny droplets decorating her shoes. I imagine some supernova event through which the light of a billion years passes through me. *Neutrinos are massless. They pass through you without your noticing. A million neutrinos could pass through you in a minute.*

She asks, *And you?*

Being honest, I don't much like school either. My school is in Dublin; I board. I think the school has a mission to minimize imagination. I get in trouble a lot, through not paying attention, not coming to class. I get bullied a bit; I guess they feel that I am kinda different. There are few places where I can go out on my own. My only privacy is a quick cigarette behind the bicycle shed. Everything is regulated. You have your regulation bed, your regulation blanket, a regulated bathroom, regulated classes. I guess it is a kind of war against intelligence. Intelligence is a threat. Because intelligence asks questions. And we are supposed to be regulated. We are not supposed to ask questions. And we are always supposed to support the school. Like following the school rugby team. After lunch we crowd into the gym. We practice rugby match songs. It reminds me of some sort of Nuremburg rally. Then we get buses to muddy sports fields. I stand in the mud that oozes through my shoes (we always arrive about 2 hours early) watching bad rugby being played by people I do not like at all such as the sixth former who, when he was in fourth form and I in second, used to make me clean his shoes and once forced me to eat three cigarettes when he caught me smoking. And another sixth former who, when he was in third form and I in first, pulled my thumb until it went crack. I had to wear a splint for a month. It's still not quite right. Sometimes I manage to escape by hiding in the toilets. The food is inedible. One has regulation anonymous meat served in filthy aluminum dishes with a layer of regulation brown gunk and regulation greasy stuff and when you stir these up you get meat in gravy. After each meal, the remaining food is taken away by some of the juniors. The milk has all sorts of stuff in it; for some reason it is considered creative to put bits of fries, bits of eggs, into the milk jugs. The milk jugs are then poured into a vat through a sieve, and are then reserved for the next day. Obviously the milk is perpetually sour. I don't have a Caribbean island but I read. And I draw. When I am drawing I escape. I can draw anything and be that. I can draw the teachers and the people I dislike, covering the drawings with swastikas. I can express myself without anyone judging me, anyone marking me, anyone sending me to detention or making me do penance for perceived disrespect to a senior. I keep my drawings under the bed. Also, there is some maths I've been working on. I have an interest in something called asymptotes. I won't bore you. One finds these little ways of escaping ... After class, I go behind the bicycle shed and have a cigarette. I breathe the smoke into my lungs and then breathe it out slowly. I feel the tension of the day dissipate. I concentrate on the sun and raise my head upwards. The school, the bullies, float away into the ether. For a small moment, just a few minutes, I feel that I exist. Really exist. I do not exist in class. I certainly don't exist in mealtimes. Or when playing sport. I exist only when I can make the school rise up and disappear. I breathe in the smoke and I am in touch with something. Something real. Something beyond the regulation day turning you into a nicely regulated human being. A human being that does not ask questions. A human being that becomes an accountant. A human being that joins the past pupil's union. A human being that is married with 2.5 children and goes on holiday once a year to Spain. A human being that drives a Mondeo and goes out with his office chums on a Friday night. In my brief moments of escape I can be what I want to be. I can be free. Freedom exists. One finds it in the small corners of life where no one can see you ... I sometimes dream that I am on a train traveling through Europe, that I watch the countryside spread out before me and small towns appearing only to disappear again. And no one knows where I am. No one can contact me. I am there in complete solitude, moving with the motion of the train, moving through the fields that appear through the window. Moving through each reality and each dream time. Existing. Not existing. Existing most because I am not existing ... My teachers want me to go to Cambridge. In a way I quite like the idea. Get away from everything I know. Away from the boring routines at home. Father reads the paper and then settles down for the afternoon with whiskey and the television. He goes to sleep. Then he wakes up blearily and goes to bed. Mother seems to be perpetually washing up. As there are only three of us, I find it hard to understand where all the washing up comes from. But she seems to take it as the testament to her existence. I wash up, therefore I am. I wash up to be. I be to wash up. One finds small reasons to exist, and small reasons not to exist. One finds a way of burying oneself under the accumulated clutter of one's life. One keeps a red book of memories in the cupboard and leaves it there without looking at it ...

The   Spark

Of   Existence

Is   Born

Through   The   Weaving

Of   One's   Mind

2

Walking through a field of barley ... the ears glisten in the sun and make a rustling sound in the breeze. I feel them with my hands, like sense, like a realization of all that there is. Mary laughs, running through the field as a testament to her own freedom ... a hawk hovers in the sky, looking for a mouse or something; its stillness seems mesmeric. I point it out to Mary and she looks. She says that the bird is *life, stillness and waiting*. We catch the moments as they hover above making subtle little movements in the stillness.

We reach the lake. We lie down underneath a tree. The birds sing above us, creating their own hymn to the universe. The water sparkles in the sun.

It's so still here ...

Yes, I come here when I need to be still. When I need to check out of everything ...

Life moves softly through the branches. I say to Mary that if I go to college I would like to study philosophy.

Why?

Because sometimes I feel that thinking is all there really is. I mean, one could imagine reality as a given fact. Like Father, the television and the whiskey. And we never look beyond that fact. That fact is all there is. And we are trapped. We can't fly. But when one goes beyond the fact as fact and emerges through the meanings behind that fact, then one begins to know that one exists. There are the two of us. There is the lake. There are the birds. This is fact. But there is more to it than that. The birds convey a message when you listen to them. The stillness of the lake forms its own meaning. The sun on the lake calls to our inspiration. The tree moves through its own history, its own coming-to-be, its own particular evolution. Everything here has grown out of its own beginnings. And through that growing, everything here has found its connection with every other thing. The tree's leaves fall into the water. There they decay and provide food for the water nymphs. These in turn provide food for the fishes and the birds. These grow up and die, each generation coming slowly through to some ultimate resolution of sense. Everything belongs to everything else. Father and the whiskey, defined by his own history, that which he evolves to be. Mother and the washing up also, we define ourselves and move through life to fit that definition. And the definition finds its own purpose. We seek that which we would come to be through the trees and the fields, through the birds, the fishes, the lake

... We scatter our definitions like confetti on the waters of the lake and watch the fishes gulp for them ... we watch them float away through their own journey, dying, and becoming, and dying again. I often wonder about Mother and the washing up. Is she trying to hide something? Some ephemeral aspiration that fades in her hands before she can realize it? Some dream that got lost through the slipstream of the cups and saucers, the greasy plates and the remnants of food stuck to the saucepans? Is she trying to find something of herself? A part of herself that is somehow lost? Is the washing up some form of elegy, a dirge towards the sense of our remembrance that brought forth the sense of our forgetting? What do we remember? What do we forget? And why? Is there a reason why we live as we do? Is there a reason why the song of the birds is not just noise, but has its own resonance? We connect and associate. And through those connections we find who we are. Father and the whiskey. Is he seeking also to forget? And if so, forget what? I lie here with you under the tree. And I look upwards. And I find your face etched through the dappled patterns that the leaves make with the sun. And I find that I hardly know you. And that I have known you for an eternity. Both. We talk of school and of being connected. Because ultimately we search for the same thing, a way to escape. A way to forget. A way to remember, and clutch those memories to our breasts as the genesis of our existence. We are. We are not. Sometimes I feel that we really

become when we lose the need to be. One can just sit. And listen to the birds. And each song they give entwines a thousand histories around it. I think of the Aborigines, the walkabout in search of the eternal songline that etches itself across the desert and defines it. We walk. We walk through the barley. And the barley whispers to us its own Rosetta Stone moment. We run our hands through it. And we imbibe its song, the silent whisper that catches us, makes us breathe. And we move through space time as people and as ghosts. Marking each moment like the quivering of the hawk, tiny movements in their stillness. We look at the calendar of life and bury each yesterday with a cross. We move through the oceans of our becoming, tasting the salt-winds as our birthing. We think. Because thinking brings freedom. If something is mere fact, then it congeals in its own immovability. If something is more than mere fact, then it transcends into its own life. We are because we think. Descartes said something like that. We are because we think, because thinking means that life transcends its stasis, forms of the moment through which our personal universes give birth to themselves and expand through us as the moment through which we catch a hundred stars in our hands and watch them be ...

Mary smiles, and the tree, the lake, the birds, smile with her. Suddenly she says *Last one in is a rotten egg ..!*

We run towards the water laughing. I just beat her. I stand waist deep in the water, my clothes sodden. Mary joins me, her wet clothes clinging to her like memory. I make a splash, and Mary does likewise. We laugh and splash each other, intoxicated by the freedom of the spontaneous, the freedom of the irrational …

Freedom is a process through which one relinquishes sense and the simple fact of things and in which one embraces that which forms of itself as random. We live through the tiny accidents that we create … I say that we had better get back now. It is getting late and parents will wonder where we are. And the wet clothes are beginning to get cold. I ask Mary if she would like to meet tomorrow, at the same time. I suggest we go back to the lake and try fishing. Mary says that she has never done that before. I tell her that it is easy when one knows how. Mary looks at me and whispers *Thank you for a wonderful day!*

I walk home, as if walking on air …

Moments

Form

The   Supernova

Of   Their   Creativity

When   Released

From   The   Confines

Of   Fact

3

I return home in my wet clothes. Mother looks up from the sink and asks me why my clothes are wet. I explain that I fell into the lake. Mother looks quizzical for a moment, says, *Oh*, and returns to peeling the potatoes. Father is watching the television with his whiskey.

Dinner is a silent affair. We eat in a sense of rapt concentration, each mouthful enjoying a profound importance that is difficult to explain. After eating, Father picks up the paper. He read it already this afternoon over lunch. But that doesn't seem to matter. He fixes on some article about taxation. His hands cause the paper to rustle slightly but apart from that, and apart from the distant yowling of a tomcat, all is quiet. I feel frozen in the moment. Like it is some sort of groundhog day that never really began and will never really end. I get up, stating that I have to do a bit of exam revision. I don't tend to revise much at the best of times. And it is a long time until I have to sit my next exam. But it gives me a reason to leave. As I leave, Mother silently gathers up the plates and moves towards the sink with them. The essential ritual of the washing up …

I lie in bed and think of Mary, and the fact that she has agreed to meet me again. The moonlight sprays silver against my window. I move through a hundred different dream states, they seem to merge with each other and become separate again. I see Mary's face under the tree, her laughter rising up like a type of hymn to the meanings that we find, the joy that sprinkles itself on the waves of our imagination like stardust …

I take my fishing rod and go out. Mary is waiting for me, wearing a loose blue summer dress and smiling broadly. We walk together to the lake, and, once there, find our tree and lie down. I place a small piece of bread on the hook and cast it into the water. A fish nibbles and I pull sharply. But the fish escapes. In some way I am glad that it did; it is nice to think of it swimming free in the lake after having narrowly escaped a sticky situation. I say to Mary *You have a go!*

I can't. I don't know how!

I'll show you. Come here. You raise the rod above your right shoulder, hold it for a count of one, and then throw it forwards … try! She tries, and the line gets tangled in a tree. *Never mind. For your first attempt that was pretty good …*

17

I take the rod again and cast into the water. I get another bite, and this time I land the fish. I kill it and gut it. Then I catch another. I smile broadly, Dinner! We gather some small sticks and light a fire. We put the fish on sticks and cook them. The smell of the fish is delicious, and the smoke rises heavenward like some sort of primordial incense to the gods. When the fish is done, we eat.

This is delicious!

Yes, it is pretty good isn't it!

We laugh at Mary's attempt at fishing and agree to do this again tomorrow, *Perhaps you will catch something.* I ask Mary for a cigarette, and we lie under the tree smoking. I breathe in deeply and feel that I am floating through some form of dappled Heaven. My mind meets with the clouds and drifts across the face of the sun like a thousand moments that have become one. Mary looks at me, her face silent as she inhales, her hair sparking drops of Jupiter in the sun. Existence moves slowly through its own dream time. A fly lands on the lake and a fish rises and gulps it down. I thought I knew freedom, but I realize that I knew nothing about it until today. We exist in that silent closeness through which all realization gives birth to itself and ascends into the cosmos of its own dreaming. We move softly through the ages. I get out the fishing knife and carve *Mary and John* on the trunk of the tree. I explain that the tree will keep the memory of the day for as long as it grows, and that as it grows the memory will expand. I look at Mary and ask what she is thinking …

Dreams flow through life. I feel like I am on my island, although not really, because I am here. I am thinking of home, and making cups of tea for my brothers when I get in. I am thinking of college. I am thinking of school. And yet I am not really thinking about these things. I am thinking of one tiny moment in spacetime. One moment that scatters the light of the sun and sings to the quicksilver of the moon. I am thinking that everything is frozen here and yet it moves, it breathes, it is alive. And I catch that life in my hands as if it were a butterfly, all fragile, and then I let it go. I watch it rise towards the sky and glisten in the blue. I watch it get smaller and smaller, and then disappear. And when it disappears, I hold the memory of it. And because I have the memory of it, it is still with me, still floating above my head and whispering of the nature of happiness. And I am thinking about happiness. The moment through which one's soul soars towards the clouds and shimmers in their whiteness. The seagull that floats over the beaches of its beginning, the flow and whisper of the barley in the wind. A thousand things becoming one thing, and then the one thing shattering into sunlit sparks that dance through one's life and call you in the nighttime to get out of bed and look at the moon, just look at it. The dream becomes real and the real becomes dreamlike. And we are a thousand different people from one day to the next and yet the same person. The person who goes to school and stares out the window during Irish class. The person who tidies the kitchen and makes her brothers cups of tea when they get home from work. And yet with all that, one is the person who flies with the birds across continents, the person who no one can coerce. My island is freedom. This is freedom. Sitting by the lake. Smoking. Breathing it all in. Moving through the eons that defined ourselves before we met. Moving through each meeting place, each silent moment when life comes and whispers to us. Each distant star and the closeness of the coming together, the coming together with you, the lake, the birds, the taste of the trout and the sparks of the fire that rise up like some sort of prayer. I hold this day in my memory, this perfect day, this endless day …

We gather ourselves together and go home. I ask Mary whether her parents will wonder where she has been. She looks me and half smiles. She says nothing.

Moments   Sing

The   Songs

That   Form

The   Sparks

That   Form

Of   Our   Existence

4

We decide to meet at the gate of the field that leads to the lake at 3pm each day. During the course of the morning it is hard to think of anything else. I watch the birds through the window, calling through their language of song, their language of remembering and forgetting. I move through the silent lunchtime like I am separate from it, yet part of the universe that carves its beginning through the trees and the lake, the dappled sun on the ground and on Mary's hair, the light splintering through it like the supernova through which our meanings shatter themselves across the nights of our freedom, moving through the closeness of holding hands and looking at each other, and through the closeness and the distance that we form in each tiny movement through the beginnings through which we rise like incense, rise like the sparks from the fire as they scatter heavenward when I poke the fire with the stick (and Mary is getting better at fishing). I think of school and the regulation meals, the regulation bed and the life that only finds its meaning through containment. And then the thoughts of school evaporate like subliming iodine and fizzle out in the sun as it sparks its own peculiar art through its shattering on the water of the lake. We find a silence that resonates through all communication, that exists as we hold hands, that exists as we breathe out our lives in a symphony of exhilaration that forms out of a dirge to the beginnings of creation, out of which existence gives birth to itself and then gives birth to itself again, etching its story across the beginning of everything. I know that through each end beginning is formed, and we wrap our hands against that beginning just in case it escapes ... and when we find our oneness with that beginning, we release it from our hands and watch it fly delicately, like a butterfly, its shimmering wings moving through the breathing in which we find our lives again ... existing through the moments that we capture and set free, and through the distance that calls us to our closeness. Watching Mary lying under a tree, her hair glinting and her face looking upward as if caught in some conversation with a galaxy that spins a million light years from us and yet is with us, the oscillating spiral of a thousand imaginations that find their resolution in this moment, this silent, sacred moment through which all is quiet and whispering, even the birds seem to whisper to us, inviting us into their sense of being. A bird swoops across the lake and picks up some insect. The insect has laid its eggs and moves from the water in its final dance before oblivion ... the endless cycle of life moving through the drumbeat of each minute where we exist and don't exist. The flittering thought that moves through our minds and weaves within us its own filaments. Mary's face … etched through some ancient time when we had not yet discovered the sophistications that distract us, before capitalism, and Thatcher, and the material world. A time when we could breathe without the screech of cars. Time is frozen in a moment, the moment that catches its light through Mary's hair, that moves with her chest as she breathes in, out, a smile slowly forming on her face as she lies there, a thousand silent thoughts rising through her breathing. Images move through the times when we can touch the stillness, the silk-woven forgetting, and the times when I imagine holding her hand and oscillating wildly through the Milky Way, nothing touching us, and we only touching each other. I imagine holding her hand and floating through the still blackness of the universe, playing games with the stars as we move within and without of each other, the quick, quick slow, of a thousand dances too ancient to remember, the escape that rushes through our veins like exhilaration and yet sings softly in its stillness … WE ARE … I run my finger through her hair and her eyes open lazily. *What are you thinking?*

She looks at me, her head rising slightly. *I'm not sure really. Just being here. Being with you. Looking up at the sun – with your eyes closed you just get this pink light. I imagine myself a million miles from here. And I imagine myself here. I drift from self to self. I had an image of my Irish teacher, her face permanently frozen in an expression of disapproval. I imagine the island. I imagine each moment sparking off the lake in kaleidoscopic cacophony and yet silent. I breathe the silence in. I breathe the silence out. Then a bird sings and the silence evaporates. And then I am here. And I am with you. I am here and yet I am everywhere. I am at school. I am staring out the window watching a bird sing a song in celebration of its freedom. I am one. And I am a thousand things. Through being a thousand things, I am one. I am alone. And yet I am with everyone. I am with the class. I am on the island. I am in Dublin watching the cars as they shriek past, and the junkies on the street eyes fixed in mesmerized desperation. I move through the litter that spirals in the wind eddies that twirl through the road as the cars go by. I am everywhere. Because I am here. And because I realize that being here is the beginning of all freedom. Freedom exists when you silently embrace it, when you allow its song to reach into you, when you become ...*

She smiles, and then lies down again. Each element of us catching its own rhythm through her breathing, through the beating of the birds' wings as they flit through the skies of imagination, reaching out to the clouds and brushing them with their wings. Time is frozen. Frozen in Mary's breathing. The Big Bang scatters the universe before us and we reach out across the sky and touch it. We find infinity in our breathing and wrap its threads around our fingers, moving through the slowness … I breathe in. I try to hold my breath for as long as possible. And then I breathe out again. I breathe in again, holding my breath. I feel nothing other than Mary beside me and my breathing … I levitate somewhere between my reality and the beginning of everything, that edge of existence which is born and dies and then is born again. I walk through the songlines of ages, letting the Great Spirit flow through my fingers like sand.

The   Images

We   Form

Paint

Their   Graffiti

Across   The   Walls

Of   Our   History

5

I move through the distance that created us
I move through, your hand in mine, twirling through the
nothingness that gave birth to our existence, we
Scatter ourselves on the ground of our dreaming, we
Move through each beating song the image of the bird in flight,
we
Catch the figments through which we are and we come to
be, moving through the Echoes through which our existence
resonates against the rocks, we
Move through the salt-spray birthing of the waters upon the
face of the cliffs as we exist over and over, we
Hold hands and spin through the Infinite moment through
which we are and come to be, we
Motion through our Being as the sun scatters its meaning on
the waters of the lake as we
Move through the kitten-soft moment through which we
become of each other and blend into the fabric of our

dreaming, we

Dance through a thousand universes that gave birth to
themselves across the interface of our imagining, we
Raise our faces to the glinting sunlight and offer our songs to
the beginnings through which we were born and die, only to be
born again, we

Wander through the distant histories whose explanations
carve themselves on the face of the Rock of Ages, we
Link fingers and move through the stratosphere, we
Shimmer in the supernova moment where dreams begin only
to evaporate in the stillness and move through the mirrors of
what we come to be.

6

I wait as I usually do. But Mary is late. After waiting an hour, I decide to go home. Mother is at her washing up, and Father in front of the television with his whiskey. I don't say much, just go up to my room and lie on my bed, staring at the ceiling hoping for some form of resolution. I pick up a book and look at it lazily; I do not feel very interested in reading it. I try and do a bit of drawing. I draw Mary, with her red hair blowing in the wind and the kind of dreamy expression she always had when she was lying at the shore of the lake, her face tilted towards the sun ...

I am called to dinner. Mother brings one of her stews and a plate of boiled potatoes and hands us our food, moving through her silence like a ghost. Father picks up the paper and reads as he eats, the rustling of the pages the only sound apart from a dog barking in the distance. I look through the windows at the stillness outside. Movements, slowly motioning through to memories and forgetting. I explain that I am tired and need to go to bed early.

Mother and Father are most often in bed by 10. I lie on my bed and wait until about 10:15 and then open my bedroom window carefully. There is creeper on the walls of the house. I inch my way out of the window slowly, being careful not to make any noise (although Mother and Father most often sleep deeply). The moon casts its silver across the lawn. A vixen moves through the shadows, her eerie call splitting the night like memory. We are. We are not. I imagine Mary's face, turned towards the sky, her eyes shut, drifting through her thoughts, moving through to the shimmering clouds of her imagination. A dog barks in the distance. I wonder if it is the same dog as over dinner. I reach the ground and set off down the avenue. Each footstep seems to take an age. An owl hoots its elegy to the night. Apart from that, silence wraps around me like a cloak.

I walk two miles, maybe three. Eventually I reach Mary's house and throw a stone at her bedroom window. The window opens and I see her face, framed like a painting in the moonlight.

Mary, it's me!

John?

Yes!

Wait a bit, I'll try to come down.

She comes out of the window, and stands in front of me, silent, but with tears in her eyes.

What happened?

One of my brothers said that he saw me with you. My father went mad. He hit me and told me not to go out. Said I was good for nothing …

I look at her face. One of her eyes is black and there is a bruise on her left cheek. I say that I am sorry. She says that it is going to be difficult to see me but we will manage, somehow. She takes me by the hand and we walk down the road together. We find an old barn and lie down together. We move through each other's breathing. We touch Infinity slowly. We move through the drumbeat of a thousand lives. We join together, merging into each other. We live some distant resolution that formed through the song that sung-in the necessity of our being. We touch slowly, moving into the togetherness that called to us, called to us through some distant desert landscape where our songs began and where we moved through the spiral-dance of history, history's sand filling our tea cups with the remnants of its dreams. We motion together in the form of that moment when all sense becomes nonsense and all nonsense sense. We move through each stage of being, evolving together like the song of its distance. We are one. And nothing else exists. We form our resolution here, breathing silently together as the stars seem to shine just for us and the moonlight slinks under the door like a thief. The form of each description paints itself wildly through the universe of our senses. The edge of everything crinkles in our hands ...

I walk Mary back to her house. She looks at me and touches my mouth with her finger. She climbs through her bedroom window.

I move on home.

I have never felt so connected.

I have never felt so utterly alone.

Images

Of   Ourselves

Condense

In   The   Moonlit   Moments

Where

We   Finally

Cease

To   Be

7

When we touch I feel a million ages, caught between your
hand and mine. We
Move to that distant place where we learn to come to be
In your eyes I see a hundred histories spiralling towards the
songline of their dance.
When I remember you, your face turned to the sun as if in
silent prayer, I
Catch my meaning and watch it bleed on the walls that divide
us, when I
Remember the silence that moves through to the rhythms of
the symphonies through which we
Celebrated the universe that we created through the beating of
the wings that took our dreams soaring to
The azure blue sky of liquid belongings, we
Moved through the caves created by millennia, we
Sprayed our beings' sea salt upon the rocks and touched the
spray with our fingers, we

Moved through the time when silence resolved itself through
the tiny drops that run down the windows of our lives like
tears, we
Live to remember against the forgetting that forces itself upon
us like some
Dictator that moves so as to define us through him, the
Call of the birds and that irrepressible freedom that was born
each time you smile, that
Exists through the carved rock moment of some ancient
civilization that gives testimony to the gods in their wildness,
that
Moves through the time where we were set free only to find
ourselves captive again, I
Feel the prison of my confinement but yet you manage to
shatter it, your
Smile casting a thousand redemptions that glisten in the
moonlight and fall like soft rain against the barriers between
us, moving
Slowly through the fact of my transcendence, the
transcendence that gave birth to itself in the liquid blue of
your eyes.

8

Back to school. The regulation lifestyle. Preparations for Leaving Certificate and possibly university. I stare out the window thinking of the lake, the birds, the sparkle of the water and shards of sunlight in Mary's hair. I draw pictures of her when I am supposed to be concentrating on Maths. I think of her when I lie down and go to sleep. Her face, her smile, her liquid blue eyes. Images of freedom that one reaches to catch only to find they are ephemeral and dissolve as soon as one touches them. The cacophony of radios. The routine of classes. Slipping out for a quick cigarette to form a few precious minutes of escape. One exists like this. Each day the same as the last. Images of freedom fading under the regime of school mealtimes. Moments of relief only to be shattered by the raucous shouting of rugby matches. I try to write:

Dear Mary,

I think of you often. I think of your smile and the freedom we found by the lake. I imagine I am there when sitting in class. I imagine I am there when attempting to eat the inedible school food. As I exist in the meaningless routine of days, I imagine running through the barley with you, the sun sparking on your hair. I imagine floating through the sky and describing histories with my fingers, your eyes singing a thousand songs, in some vain comfort for the loneliness I feel now. Everything here is routine. I long to break out, to go somewhere, to do something different … I imagine running with you through the desert that life can be, singing in the sun a thousand movements, creating symphonies with our laughter. I am supposed to be studying for exams. But I find it hard to concentrate. One of the students here sells contraband vodka. His father is some form of diplomat and travels a lot, so he has access to Duty Free (I think it is some form of compensation for his parents neglecting him). I find some comfort with this. At least it removes some of the routine. We sit, and drink, and smoke cigarettes. And your image comes into my mind. I reach out and try to touch it. I sometimes think of quantum mechanics, that ultimately reality is driven more by probability than certainty. I don't know exactly why, but I find that to be a comfort. That there are no immutable absolutes, but instead probabilities and relations. I read a book about Relativity Theory. It says that even time itself is not immutable but instead depends on relations. One can even travel into the future ... With the vodka, I can break for a while the absolutism of routine. There is no lake here; there are very few areas where one can be alone. Other people crowd in on you, muscling in on your space, catching you ... I think of you when I look at the sky at night. Each star you see you are actually seeing millions of years ago. I don't know why, but I find that to be a comfort too. Like we are not fixed. That we can move through life in a process of creativity rather than stasis. I remember us imagining that we were spiralling through the Milky Way, playing with the universe with our fingers ... They say that freedom is within. It can be. But freedom has to exist outside of oneself as well. Here, I find it hard to connect. The routine crushes one. I think that ultimately that is the intention. I comfort myself through knowing that my exams will come soon and then I will be leaving here. I comfort myself most of all through believing that I will see you again.

J.

I don't know whether she got the letters I wrote. I rush to post every morning looking for something, but there is nothing. I go to class. Decline an Irish verb. Do some calculus. Drink some vodka. Passing time. I cross out each day on my calendar, nearer to release. Nearer to Mary. I eat the school food in silence. I form my own antidote to routine. I look at the sky at night and imagine dancing with Mary through the cosmos. I get up the next day. I go to post. Nothing. I decline an Irish verb. Routine can in itself be intoxicating. It precludes everything else. When one submits to routine the pain abates. Routine numbs, it is an anaesthetic. I think of Schrödinger's Cat. Alive and dead at the same time until someone opens the box. I feel like that. Both alive and dead. I long for some assurance that I am alive – the shards of light in the red hair, the liquid blue of Mary's eyes – just to know I am not dead. Just to know that the routine hasn't killed me. Even though I wish sometimes that it would. Existing and moving. Moving through the geometries of our disconnect. Embracing the disconnect because there is nothing else. I disconnect. Therefore I am not. Therefore I am ...

Drifting

Through

The   Images

We   Define

At   The   Edge

Of   Our   Despair

9

I go to post. There is a letter. Mary's handwriting. My heart skips a beat and I feel a rush in my veins. I open it.

Dear John,

I don't know if you will get this. I haven't received any letters from you, but I suspect that you do write and that my parents confiscate them. I don't know how to say this, but I have missed a couple of periods. Life here is lonely. My parents are furious with me and have grounded me. I go to school, and they pick me up afterwards and I have to stay in the house. I help Mother with the housework and continue to make cups of tea for my brothers. I sometimes look at the birds outside the window – life is so much easier for them. They don't have to conform. They don't have to be respectable. They don't get gossiped about by the neighbours. School is boring. My parents say they won't support me going to university, so it makes no difference how I do in my exams. I stare out the window and look at the picture of the Caribbean island trying to teleport myself so I can be free. I'm just passing time. I go to bed and I look up at the ceiling. Sometimes it is as if it were revolving round and round. I try to stop it with my hands. I cry silently, then get up, do the breakfast for everyone and am taken to school by my parents. At school, everyone has their own agenda. But I have one friend, Eileen, who I hope will post this letter to you. If you want to write, I have enclosed her address. I remember fishing by the lake. The peace. The sense of escape. That I am a real person. That I am alive. I hope to find that again, somehow.

M.

I move through the song of ages. I am delighted that she got in touch. And I am sad also. I feel a type of guilt, that I made all of this happen. I do the routine thing. Irish verbs, calculus, vodka, cigarette, more vodka. I move through quick, quick slow. I search for the moments that I feel I have lost somehow. I draw at the back of the class. I am reading something to do with superstring theory. I find the comparative surreality comforting, that matter is a small string and the actual particle depends on the resonance of the string because the resonance gives the string energy. And mass and energy are equivalent. I imagine that we are all little strings, resonating and forming of our own particular realities. I am a pion. You are a meson. We are defined by our resonance. And if we change our resonance, I can become you and you can become me. I like the idea that space might have 12 dimensions, but most of these dimensions are imperceptible because they are curled around each other. I don't know why, but I find that comforting too, that we are eternally precluded from ever perceiving the entirety of reality save through some mathematical equations, that there will always be something hidden, some secret, a code we cannot break. I imagine loads of dimensions curled around each other, permanently hidden until some mathematician comes up with the requisite formula. I imagine we are like that too. We cannot entirely define ourselves. We just create formulae through which we hope to find some explanation for our existence. 'Me' is defined through some squiggles on a white board in a Cambridge University Particle Physics department. I am lines and symbols, lines and symbols. I am an asymptote that predicts the form of me but ultimately defines nothing. We are defined by four dimensions, three of space, and one of time. But our reality exists separate from that format. Our reality is born when we cease to have any reality at all. I am a Klein bottle, a Möbius strip. My beginning has no end save from my beginning. I exist in the abstractions that deny the fact of my existence. I am the 12th dimension. I am imperceptible. I am … through ceasing to be.

Drifting   Through

The   Images

We   Make

We   Find

The   Calculus

Of   Our   Silent

Cry

To   Nothing

10

Leaving Certificate done. I walk out the school gates, looking back once. The end of routine and the beginning of … I look forward to getting home, to seeing Mary. I catch the train, watching the landscape flow past me and through me like dreaming … I light a cigarette and breathe in deeply … The sun glints off the window like memory, I see the sparks of light that would glisten in Mary's hair … We reach the station and Father is there … He doesn't say much, I feel an incipient disapproval. He takes one of my bags and we walk towards the car. He drives in a manner that seems compulsive, eyes fixed in front like obsession. We get home and the dog greets me. I put my arms around him and he licks my face in some sort of compensation for the lack of welcome.

We get home and Father pours himself a whiskey and retreats to the television room. Mother stands at the sink with her ritual of washing the dishes. She doesn't say much, but hands me a cup of coffee. Welcome. I look at Father's whiskey. I wouldn't mind a drink myself but know that it is better not to ask him. I decide to go for a walk …

I walk through the fields to the lake where I had sat so often with Mary. I imagine her laughter, her attempts at fishing. I throw a stone into the water and watch the ripples fan out like the songs of my memory. I lie in the summer sun and listen to the birds twittering images through the stillness of the now dark green leaves. The solitude wraps itself around me like some form of comfort blanket. I wrap my arms around my body for warmth, reassurance. I feel like I am spinning with ghosts and phantoms, and rising up to the memory of Mary's laughter …

I return home. I ask Mother, who has just prepared dinner and hands it out to the three of us, some form of beef stew that she often makes with lumps of meat and potato, I ask, *Is Mary O'Reilly still working here?*

Mother and Father stare at me, their gaze fixated like ice. *No.*

Will she be coming back?

No.

Mother and Father appear to attack their food. The knives and forks clatter against the plates like aggression. No one says anything, just the clatter, clatter, and fixed stares across the table. I feel uncomfortable and ask if I can leave the table.

Father shakes his head and tells me to wait until everyone is finished. He picks up the paper and opens it angrily. I ask again if I can leave. He says, 'No'. I point out that he has finished eating. He says that he said no, and no is no. I sit like this for about 20 minutes, chasing a small piece of potato around my plate for wont of something to do. Then I get up. No one says anything. I go to my room and put on my Walkman. I listen to a song by *Sonic Youth* that appears to be about dinner parties ... *Here we go to another candlelight blow ... They're talking all right but it's just sherry-o* ... I remember sitting at a table with 20 others, all talking, no one saying anything, a million conversations competing around the candlelight as they fight to be heard. And Mary ... Mary by the lake with the sun in her hair. I don't know what is worse, the silence, the silence that sticks to you like a London afternoon in the heat, or the conversations, each one the same, each one finding its meaning through the fulfilment of its ultimate monotony. I get up and go downstairs. I tell Mother and Father that I am going out. They say nothing. I lie on my back on the lawn, eyes heavenward, counting the stars, their light calling to me across millions of years. It takes the light that amount of time to reach us. I imagine time traveling, oscillating between past and future. I imagine going from planet to planet and on each planet finding the lake, the birds, Mary's hair. I hear the hoot of an owl in the distance describing its own elegy. I move within myself and around myself, spinning wildly in the bitter sweet song of my dreaming. I feel the dampness of the grass beneath me as I slowly slip into a world of my own creation, a world where we begin and end to begin again, a world where the hymns of our dreaming sing sweet music to the sense of our remembrance and our forgetting, breathing in, out, catching the joy, and sadness, that echoes through our lives and in our beating hearts ...

The   Images

Of   Our   Meaning

Compose

The   Music

Of   Our   Senses

11

We move through the images that we make of us,
The gentle rose buds of our thoughts tingling our fingers, I
move through you, within you and without you, our
Dreams chasing through the crashing of the waves of our
birthing, I
hold your hand and I am a million people and yet,
I am alone with you, I
write your name and my name in the sand and watch the
waves wash over and carry us to the azure blue of Eternity, I
Move through the whispered moments when we said so much
without speaking, our
Linked fingers creating a million songs that rise up as incense
to the Gods of our being, I
move through the sway of the grass and the smell of the
honeysuckle on the gates to your house, I
wait for you in the distant moments when we steal a meeting, I

Motion through my breathing, each meeting, each moment,
each memory, each dream …

12

I take to walking. I walk to the lake. Through the village. Sometimes I have a pint in one of the pubs even though I am not supposed to. Father says that They drink in pubs. I never really understood this thing about Them but I was brought up to believe that it was something to be avoided. We associate with Us; They associate with Them. Some sort of historical neurosis that is clung onto in the hope that it might confer some sort of meaning and importance. We have dinner parties and exchange anecdotes; They drink in pubs. I remember reading a poem, I think by Robert burns, A man's the same for all that … I never saw the point of deliberate isolation. Mary was one of Them. And Mary had more life in her than the endless recycled conversations that went on only where they'd been before …

One of my walks takes me by Mary's house. I move to her gate in the hope of her seeing me. I spot a hand wave.

John? Is it you? Suddenly the universe sparks into some glistening celebration. She moves to the gate. *We'll get in real trouble if my parents see you here!*

I couldn't keep away for any longer. I had to come. How are you?

Fine. Missing you. The lake. The fishing! My parents don't like me going out. I fix the dinner. I do the housework. I bury each day with a cross on my calendar. I draw pictures. Sometimes I sing 'It's so lonely round the fields of Athenry.' Sometimes I cry myself to sleep. Sometimes I laugh, though at what I am not sure. But laughter shatters the loneliness. The loneliness is worst at night, in the silence. The silence whispers an end to dreaming, an end to life. It wraps its darkness around my body and suffocates me. It is really great to see you ... I sometimes go to the shop to buy cigarettes for my brother. Usually at about 3pm. Meet me at the hedgerow beside Mr. O'Connor's place. We won't have long, but we can steal a meeting ...

I reach to the ground and pull up a dandelion. Its yellow seems to offer hope. A spot of colour. I hand it to her, *For you.*

And we agree to meet at 3pm.

Drifting   Through

The   Images

We   Paint

Of   Ourselves

On   The   Walls

Of   Our   Lives

13

It is about 2:30pm and the silent ritual of lunch is over. Mother scrapes the remnants from the plates into a composting bin and Father pours himself a whiskey and heads to the television room. I say that I am going out. Nothing is said. I say that I will take the dog out for his walk. Mother says okay. Father says nothing. I get the lead and go out the door.

I feel a strange mix of exhilaration and sorrow. There is a misty rain that dampens my hair. It is refreshing. The dog thoroughly enjoys smelling around the road. I get to Mr O'Connor's gate. It's about 2.45. I feel songs and tears, both. I light a cigarette and breathe in, out, in, out, forming my sense of myself through the smoke. I find an echo of myself in the rain, the cigarette, the sole bird that proclaims its territory like it owns the place. I feel lightheaded, my mind floating through the rain and through the song of that lone bird, catching its dirge through the loneliness of ages ... I do not know whether she will turn up. I look at my watch again. And again. I hear footsteps and look down the road ...

We throw our arms around each other. We are laughing, crying, both. I touch her face with my fingers and feel a thousand infinities flow through them, through her, through me. She explains that she can only be five minutes or so; her parents will wonder what had kept her. I touch her hair gently and she touches mine. It seems like forever caught in a moment, forever beating its rhythm through our hearts and lifting us through the sky and carrying us through a million moments that give birth to themselves in the shimmer-silver of the dream time song when all that is apart comes together. When the silences that exist between us explode into a symphony of joy, breaking through our lives like the sun through the rain and shining warmth on our faces like all the songs of hope and the dance through which we catch history by the hand and float upwards, glinting like the sparks of the primordial fire that gave birth to our being ... Mary and I hold hands and dance on the road. I catch her spinning, her hair waving in the breeze, and her laughing, laughing at all that brings us together and separates us, the dance of a hundred ages that forms its genesis through our hands holding together, a freedom that shatters housework, the dinner party, school, all the routines that are created to trap us, to stop us being who we really are ... And as we dance I feel that reality, the sense of self, that holding onto Life with all its ups and downs, sweetnesses and disappointments ... I notice she is crying and I touch her cheek with my finger. She smiles softly, the rain making her skin shine like silk ... Everything exists in this moment, the entire Cosmos condensed into one little moment of time, one little moment when freedom breaks through all the confines that we create around ourselves, the definitions and the refutations through which we are told what we must be, what they say we must become ... Each echo moves through the dance and the laughter, a million beginnings that fly through our minds like the wings of a golden eagle that soars, untameable, answerable to no-one, of itself and of itself only, regardless of the wills of others, regardless of the definitions they use to snare us, regardless of the values of a society that refutes us the day we are borne, regardless of the silence and the aggression, the crashing of the cutlery against the plates in some kind of war against life ... life which holds us and beckons us into the flight of a million birds into the golden sunset and the greeting of the shimmering sunrise of our being.

The   Flights

Of   Our   Freedoms

Sparkle

Through   The   Moments

Through   Which

We   Find

What   It   Is   To   Be

14

Those perfect moments when we spin together echoing through
the rooftops the songs of our flight, I
Move with you through the slipstream and the desert, we
Meet at the interface of time, breathing each moment at the
beginnings of our coming to be, I
Echo in my heartbeat the rhythm of our dancing, we
Move quick, quick, slow through the dawn of our becoming, we
Create over and over, moulding universes through our fingers.

15

Through the summer we meet like this, stealing little moments. Sometimes she is there, sometimes I know she can't make it. Mother and Father expand in their silence the resentment that slips ghost-like through each room in the house. I walk a lot, taking the dog out. The dog is glad of the exercise. His tail wags. It must be great to be a dog. Life is so comparatively simple. And even an old stick is fun. Sometimes we go to the lake together. I dip my hand in the water and look at my reflection. Mary's seems to be there too sometimes, with that wonderful glint of sunshine in her hair. Sometimes I throw a stick in for the dog to retrieve. He leaps into the water in delight. I will be going to university soon. In some way I am relieved, it will get me away from here, the memories, the phantoms that stalk my mind in the night time. In some way I am sad, those stolen moments with Mary, I will miss them terribly. Mary and I agree to communicate through Eileen. I notice that Mary's stomach is getting bigger …

I pack up my things. I don't have much. A few clothes, some

tapes, a tape player, a kettle, some text books and a picture of Mary. Father comes upstairs and calls me. I bring my case downstairs and we drive to the airport. Father says nothing through the journey. His hands clench at the wheel and he drives fast (something he often does, particularly when he is angry). I stare out the window watching home with all its familiarities, all its pain and all its joy, retreat. I light a cigarette and open the window. I offer Father one; he occasionally smokes. But he doesn't say anything …

We arrive at the airport early. Father drops me off and heads straight back. I check in and wander about. I don't much like airports; I have a neurosis that I will get through security only to find that I have lost my passport and my boarding card and am consequently stuck, trapped. I decide to go to the bar and have a pint, maybe two pints. People seem to be transfixed in some eternal anonymity. They wander around like refugees from themselves, drifting through the sort of stateless feeling one has when one feels one belongs nowhere and yet everywhere at the same time. There are some people obviously off on sunshine holidays. They have oversized sun hats and cases bulging with various forms of sun cream and irritated children who insist on running about everywhere to relieve themselves of boredom. Some are obviously businessmen; small cases and newspapers. All humanity seems to be here vying for identity among the check-out desks and the shops selling overpriced sunglasses; some are finding their names and identities in the departure and arrival notices, some are going, some coming back, some are waiting, some are meeting others ... I sit at the bar and watch them, as if I am studying them, as if I am doing a PhD in anthropology centring around the cultural dynamics of airports. I begin to quite enjoy the sense of statelessness, the feeling of not belonging anywhere but in this particular moment, this constant procedure of nowhere ... I light a cigarette and move through the crowds in my mind, through them all, between them all, touching everybody and touching nobody, moving through the miasma of drifting lives that seem to condense in my pint, moving through me like ghosts, neutrino people who pass through you without you, or they, noticing. A hundred lives that intersect for that split second before dissolving in the face of the man at security gate who frisks you ...

There is a delay at the gate. A businessman (identifiable through his briefcase and his newspaper) looks constantly at his watch, face creased in irritation. An elderly couple share a copy of *The Sun*, something about Princess Diana. It appears that there is always something about Princess Diana. I wonder what it would be like to be her, every mistake, every fallibility broadcast to the world by Murdock. Has she had an affair? Is she bulimic? Does she take Prozac? I am not terribly touchy-feely about royalty but I feel for her. The lonely face that gets photographed everywhere she goes, the face trying to smile for the camera but concealing pain, every act of kindness translated into some form of propaganda for something she ultimately doesn't believe in. I think she is genuinely kind, just caught up in something outside of her that she is forced to be. An identity construed by Murdock, an identity that is forced into its own mythology through forces she can't control … There is a family with two small children who are running about the place while their beleaguered mother shouts, *Come here! Stop it! Come here!* There is another businessman. I watch them all. For a moment they become my family. I am with these people. They are with me. Somehow we are all searching for the same thing. A destination. Somewhere to go. Because going somewhere is better than staying. If one stays one is in stasis. One becomes transfixed. One becomes the formulated phrase of others. One's volition evaporates. When one leaves one becomes answerable to no one. If one is on a plane the only others who know exactly where you are, are the other people on the plane who don't know you at all. So you are anonymous. You are free. That is the beauty of airports. I imagine I am one of those traveling salesman types. Constantly on the move. No roots. Permanently in flux. The opposite of Princess Diana who is always rooted to Murdock. Wherever she is, Murdock is there too. With me, I am at Gate No. 7. I will soon be flying over the sea. With the others. But ultimately completely separate. No one knows my name. And I don't know the names of any of the others either. But when someone sees a picture of Princess Diana, everyone knows exactly who she is, and what she is called. She is never alone. Which is why she must be so desperately lonely.

Life

Collapses

Under   The   Force

Of   Its   Imagination

16

The plane takes off. I find this part of flying both terrifying and exhilarating at the same time. I clutch onto the edge of the seat as we rise upward. I am seated next to the elderly couple with *The Sun* newspaper. The man is trying to assure his wife that she will be ok. Her eyes are closed. She appears to be praying. I take out the copy of the *New Scientist* I bought at the airport. There is something about quantum mechanics. I enjoy quantum mechanics because it stubbornly refuses to be understood. Do we go for the Copenhagen Interpretation or the Many Worlds Theory? The Copenhagen Interpretation states that we find reality when we observe it to be. The Many Worlds Theory states that with each possibility the universe splits into two, and when we observe a given outcome we find out which universe we happen to be in. I think of Mary. What would it have been like if I hadn't asked her for that cigarette? If we hadn't met? We create our own realities, and our realities create us. We dance with the universal song of being and dying. We move from reality to reality like a train going from station to station, passing through each one, catching the moment, and then leaving the moment behind for another moment ... our lives are a series of moments that seek their connection through their separateness. The moment by the lake. The moment when Mary first managed to cast the rod properly. Cooking the fish on the campfire. Tasting it. Snuggling together in the warmth of the fire. The sparks spiralling upward each time I poke the fire with a stick ... We create the moment because we exist in it. And each moment forms the weaving of our eternity, forms the cloth we put around us to ward off the cold and find our togetherness. The Copenhagen Interpretation of quantum mechanics is explained through a thought experiment 'Schrodinger's Cat.' A cat is placed in a box with a phial of poison and a radioactive isotope. If the isotope decays, the phial is broken and the cat dies. If not, the cat lives. But we don't know which, until we open the box. So is the cat alive or dead before we open the box? We can't know. So we create the reality by observing it (it's called collapsing the wavefunction). I create my realities through being able to experience them. The Many Worlds Theory states that, with the cat, when we open the box, we find out whether we are in 'alive cat universe' or 'dead cat universe.' The fact of my experience is the basis of my reality. I sit by the lake with Mary. I experience that. And through that experience I become part of a given universe. And that universe determines the future universes of which I come to be part. I see Mary at Mr O'Connor's gate. We dance. I am in that universe. And I am in that universe because I was in the universe by the lake. And I am in that universe because I asked Mary for a cigarette. We move through our experiences. We become. And through that becoming we become again. Each moment creates our existence. We move through that which determines us through our experiences, our choices, our decisions around what we want to be. The random elements also. Each random element leads us to a possible experience, a possible choice. And we make that choice because the randomness has given us the opportunity to make it. And through each opportunity we learn, we grow, we become. I am me because I sat with Mary by the lake and saw the sun glisten in her hair. I am with her. And through being with her I become me. And through being me, I am with her. We dance on the road by Mr O'Connor's gate. A stolen moment. We steal moments from the universe to become as we are. We remember, and each memory moves us through to our becoming. I remember Mary by the lake. I remember Mary dancing when we were not supposed to be together. We chose to be together because ultimately we belong to the same universe, the universe that was created by the lake, the universe that took us away from the things that restricted us. The Big Bang we formed when we first kissed …

I have a window seat. I look out at the clouds and the patchwork fields below us, and the tiny houses and cars in a separate world from me. We rise higher and we reach the coast. The sea spreads its azure below us. The clouds scatter before us. I imagine that I am in heaven, walking on the clouds, being so totally apart … The old lady seems to have recovered from her nerves and has resumed reading the newspaper. I am in the middle of the sky, totally connected, and totally disconnected. I see movement below me and yet I feel totally still. I float in a dream state and exist like some flickering particle that is itself through being something other.

We   Float   Above

Our   Realities

And   Mould

The   Beginnings

Of   Our   Dreams

17

The plane lands at Manchester Airport. The captain apologizes for the delay. The old couple gets out slowly. The whole process is mildly claustrophobic.

I wait for my luggage, collect it, and then make my way to the train. I have a place at Durham University to study chemistry. I feel tired and when on the train decide to catch a nap. The train moves off slowly. I look out the window; Manchester seems utterly unfamiliar. I have been to London once or twice but I am used to the country and find the built-up city kind of intimidating. Grey-black buildings and few green spaces. I feel a type of claustrophobia, a longing simply to run free and go wild, to jump in the lake and feel its cool waters around me. I look at the others on the train, each one lost in the throes of his or her journey, a silent communication amongst the rustle of newspapers. I buy myself a beer and light up a cigarette, watching the smoke glint against the window before disappearing in its ethereal haze. I feel ethereal myself, drifting above my body and filling the carriage with this awful sense of loneliness … I float through my memories like a phantom which seeks heaven but is just not quite able to reach it. I exist through those bittersweet moments at Mr O'Connor's gate, the stolen glimpses of happiness that one holds in one's hands before they evaporate, evaporate far too quickly … We chase our freedoms through the testaments of lives that others force us to live … I remember the dinner parties and the conversations that refuted communication … I exist in the moments that other people create for me, except for managing to steal a dream at Mr O'Connor's gate … The grey-black of Manchester turns into green fields. The hedgerows are much more manicured than they are in Ireland, as if the farmer not only wishes to farm but to control nature, to manage things … The sheep silently graze, fixed in their reality as I am in my unreality. We exist and move … Small houses with cars in front, fields, sheep … As if this was the whole of life, and the whole of what one has to escape from … I long for the chaos that enables me to be free of all of this, to be free of ordered experience. The train glides as if on air, barely making a noise, the silence embraces one, punctuated only by the rustling of newspapers. I light another cigarette and imagine its smoke as incense rising in praise to some forgotten God that asks us to connect, that asks us to disconnect, that calls through the mountains and the valleys, the sheep, the small houses, the cars and the moments at Mr O'Connor's gate, inviting us to a form of redemption that glows with the sunset of a summer evening, that scatters like the gold-shimmer leaves of autumn, that seeks itself and from thence calls on us to seek it ... I feel the universe has its own mind, seeking to communicate, inviting us to belong to it, and from thence belong to ourselves. We exist. And the existence states as its invitation 'be you and be me. Be both.' And we move through the definitions that we held as children, when life was simple, when one ran with the dogs and laughed at nothing in particular, laughed at life. Because life is a game. And it is a game that calls us ... I imagine sitting on the fence between this world and the next, translating. And my translation states that we begin and we end at Mr O'Connor's gate. We begin and end through dancing. And when we have ended enough, we begin again. We pick the honeysuckle and drink of its nectar, the sweetness playing games with our senses. We catch the birds as they flit through the air according to their own testament, catching insets to bring to their young. We are. I think of the silent mealtimes, Mother, the washing up. Father, the whiskey and the television, creating their own patterns on the interface of some cosmos that came into being when we imagined it, that echoes through the stars its own particular song to the eternity that exists through the barley and the lake, and through Mr O'Connor's gate ... We dance through the beginning of ages and find our truth through the coming together and shattering of the walls we build between us, through the realizing that *them is us and we are them,* through the form of the gentle experience of holding someone by the hand and running … running through the ties that our minds have created, running through the art that forms of all art. The coming together of a being that moves silently through the shadows of our dreaming and the exultation of our waking, breathing in and out, breathing in, and out, the smoke condensing on the train window like the last elegy to existence …

The train draws in. I get out and find a taxi to my college. I get there and unpack my stuff. I put the kettle on, brew myself a coffee, and lie on the bed looking at the ceiling. I put on a tape. The music catches me and I watch the steam rising from my coffee like a prayer. I light a cigarette and breathe in deeply, breathe out, reforming out of some sort of rhythm of sense. I am tired. I drink my coffee and then go to the dining room for something to eat. There are hundreds of other people; we are thrown together like this in one moment of time when we are made to intersect. I eat my food and then go to the college bar. I buy myself a pint of something called *Theakstons* and a whiskey chaser. There are some lads by the bar, obviously privileged given their accents. They are shouting; I find them something between threatening and really annoying. I buy another pint and put on *Absolute Beginners* on the juke box …

I absolutely love you ... and I am absolutely sane ... I think of Mary and the lake. I buy another pint, and then, feeling tired, go to bed. I lie down and my life floats before me like some ether that connects all parts of the universe with the other parts, connects all of me to myself.

Distances

Paint

Their   Meaning

As   Graffiti

On   The   Walls

Of   Our   Being

18

Lectures vary between being relatively interesting and really quite boring. I develop a liking for the lab work but a distinct dislike for organic chemistry. The evenings are spent in the student bar, or sometimes watching extremely pretentious Art House films with the Cinema Club. Things aren't nearly as regulated as they were at school, but we form our routines. I am not good around getting up for the first lecture in the morning, partly because I seem to have a constant hangover from the night before. I discover that certain colleges do 'happy hour' and one can get drinks extremely cheaply. The drink acts as an anaesthetic to the loneliness that I feel almost perpetually. I find it hard to connect with many of the others. I make one or two friends though, and we become involved in political activism. Political activism gives a sense of purpose, a sense that one can actually achieve something over and above getting such and such a mark in examinations or lab work. I take to demonstrating. I get up at about 5am (thoroughly hung over) and catch the coach from Durham to London for the purpose of shouting *Maggie! Maggie!*

Maggie! OUT! OUT! OUT! I seem to have adopted Maggie Thatcher as a type of nemesis and attempting to make that known to her gives me a meaning that was otherwise lost as soon as Mother and Father told me that Mary would not be working for them anymore. Sometimes there is trouble at the demonstrations; once or twice there are cavalry-style charges by the police. But I come to enjoy the trouble more and more. I have fun trying to get myself arrested shouting *Fascist Pigs!* at the police and waving a placard around announcing that I'm a Socialist Worker. I decided that I want to be personally responsible for Maggie being Out.

After one such demonstration, one of my friends suggests that we stay in London and visit his sister. Apparently his sister lived in a squat in Clapham. We catch the Tube (chaos through all the demonstrators) and arrive.

His sister opens the door and asks us in. There is a small gas-fired stove on which some somewhat ominous looking baked beans are bubbling. There is little furniture save a few mattresses and something that might in its distant past have been a sofa.

There are four other people who didn't look as if they had had a bath in ages.

My friend's sister rolls up a joint. I am not familiar with

cannabis (alcohol is my weapon of choice) but when passed to me I inhale deeply.

My head is spinning, the universe goes faster and faster. I grip on to what was once a sofa and feel myself levitating beyond the past, beyond the future, beyond everything ...

We stay for some time (I am not sure how long. I am floating somewhere between the Milky Way and the Magellan Cloud) and then slowly get up to go back to Durham. We get a late train. My mind is somewhere else, I feel detached from my body. My friend passes over a bottle of cheap sherry. I take a slug and put my head back and fall into an uneasy sleep ...

Images

Of   Sense

Dissolve

Like   The   Mist

That   Rises   Up

Through

The   Distant

Summer   Morning

19

I write to Mary at Eileen's address every two days. I am not sure what to tell her so I describe university life, the bars, the happy hours, the cannabis, and *Maggie! Maggie! Maggie! OUT! OUT! OUT!* I tell her that I miss her. I tell her that I think of the stolen moments at Mr O'Connor's gate all the time. I ask her how she is, what she is doing. I describe my loneliness. I write that she is the only person that ever understood me, that she is the only person I understand. I describe the boys from Harrow and Eton that appear to think they own the place, their shouting and their brutish rituals such as The Donut Run where they go to all the college bars, one after another, and drink three pints of beer in each and eat three donuts, after which they inevitably get sick and throw up. I write that my thoughts are with the cleaners who find this the following morning, and that in all likelihood, to these louts, the cleaners are Them and consequently their sensibilities are irrelevant. I describe my lectures and the fact that I have become more interested in drawing cartoons of the lecturers than taking the notes that I will need for my examinations.

Dear Mary,

I think of you often. When the sun shines, I picture you by the lake. I feel the sun on our faces, the songs of the birds create the music of our being. Life here has its ups and downs. I have decided to adopt a position of total antagonism to Maggie Thatcher and go to London once every two weeks or so to shout at her. I have made a few friends, but I am lonely here. I go to my lectures (sometimes) and go to the college bar in the evenings. They do cheap beer. Sometimes in the mornings I don't get up but lie in bed listening to the birds, as we used to.

Yours Ever,

John

The   Coming   Together

Sings

Of   A   Thousand

Goodbyes

20

I see you in the distance, the
Moon sparkling off the waters of our coming together, I
Stand on the cliff faces of our memory and imagine floating
above them, a golden eagle, I
Move through the forests of the songline through which we
etch our histories across the blank spaces that exist between
us, I
Move through the elegy of ages to hold your hand, I
Taste the sweet ambrosia on our tongues as we spiral upwards,
ever free, ever together, I
Move through the slowness through which the dawn comes to
be, each new day breaking its life across the horizon like the
thousand dreams you taught me to have.

21

Someone bangs on my door, *John? Telephone.*

I run downstairs to the public telephone. There is a voice, *John? It's Eileen. Mary's having the baby!*

I breathe heavily. I run up to my room and quickly pack a few things and then catch a taxi to the train station. I get on the next train to Manchester.

The train seems to take an age although I know it is not going any slower than normal. The countryside through the window appears hallucinogenic like some weird drug-induced experience somewhere between waking and sleeping, somewhere between living and dying. The train contains its normal mix of businessmen existing in the silent world of *The Financial Times* and day trippers reading *The Sun* or women's magazines. I light up a cigarette. And then another one. I count each breath in, out, in, out.

I arrive at Manchester and make my way from the train station to the airport. I go to the Aer Lingus desk and ask when the next plane to Ireland is, I don't mind which airport, and are there any seats available. The woman at the desk says that there is a flight in about 4 hours. There are a couple of seats available but they will be expensive as it is last-minute. I tell her I don't mind and give her the required fee.

Back in airports. The sense of belonging nowhere and everywhere at the same time. I smoke compulsively. Finishing a packet, I buy another one. I buy a puzzle book, *Logical Problems,* in the hope that it will distract me from the nervous tension that appears to be shooting relentlessly through all my bones and muscles. Existence. Non-existence. Both. I go through security and get frisked. It seems like some form of silent pantomime … to what exactly? I don't know. Everyone seems to be moving interminably slowly. The frisk seems to take an age. I go to the departure gate. Gate 7. I sit down and light up a cigarette to control the breathing which appears faster and faster. The plane is on time this time. I say a small prayer in thanks and get on. I have the window seat again. I watch us rise up heavenward like the birthing of a dream. I watch Manchester getting smaller and smaller beneath me like I own it somehow, like I cause it both to exist and disappear. We rise up into the clouds. It is a relatively clear day and one can see the ocean beneath, sparkling azure like a song.

We land. It has started to rain. I wrap my coat around me as protection from the cold. I do not have to go to luggage reclaim as I have nothing with me but a small bag. I catch a bus homeward. I decide not to let my parents know I am here and book myself into a small Bed and Breakfast run by an affable plump lady. She asks me in a Galway accent whether I would like a full Irish breakfast the following morning. I say, *Yes please*, even though I don't normally like fry ups that much, and catch a taxi to the hospital.

Outside waiting is someone I recognize as Eileen. I ask her how Mary and the baby are. Eileen looks at me slowly, *They're gone.*

What do you mean, they're gone?

Eileen says, *It was as much your family as it was hers.*

Our   Dreams

Shatter

Like   Glass

Against

The   Stone   Wall

Of   Our   Hopelessness

22

I find out that the baby was taken by the priest and put up for adoption. I find out that Mary has called him Finn.

I find out also that Mary has been taken to an institution called St. Anne's.

I have to find her.

I take a bus to Cork City. The bus is old and tatty and the radio is playing. I think of *Absolute Beginners*. The bus is mainly full of middle-aged women going into town for the day to do some shopping. We arrive at the bus station which is also old and tatty. I light up a cigarette. There is a homeless man sitting on one of the benches drinking from a vodka bottle concealed in a brown paper bag. His eyes look glazed as they slowly follow other people around. For some reason I choose to sit next to him. He smells of drink and dereliction. I offer him a smoke which he takes gladly. I give him a light, and a little bit of money also. I want to talk to him, desperately, him alone, not the others in the station. Maybe I think he will understand me. Or that I will understand him. I need connection like lifeblood. I ask him where he is from. He says, *Clare*. And, *Thanks for the smoke and the cash*. I ask him what brought him to Cork. He tells me that he became an alcoholic, lost his job and his family and wanted some sort of redemption but didn't know what. He seems at that moment to understand the entirety of human history, his glazed and watery eyes looking around him, looking at me, looking at the bottle concealed in the brown paper bag, searching for himself among the others, who he was, who he is now. I decide to give him the rest of my packet and leave, buying another before getting a taxi to St Anne's.

St Anne's rises up above the city like despair. Red brick walls and permanently closed windows. There is a nurse dressed in a white uniform in a glass box at the door. I tell her that I am visiting Mary O'Reilly. She points a finger and says, *Ward 4*.

The place smells like death. Grey paint peeling off the walls and shadow-people moving in slow-mo, roll-up fixed to lip like an indelible memory, the last memory, all that is left. They say nothing, just appear to float there like some zombie ballet constructed out of pure desolation. Nothing said. They have slippers so there isn't even the sound of shoes. Just the drift-walk, a silence that is mesmerizing in its awfulness. The doors are thick and heavy, and every so often there is a nurse carrying some kind of medication. I feel that I have come to the end of the world, some nuclear vision of a catastrophe that plays itself out in silence, the compulsive footprints of a dying civilization that speaks only to the distance of its history. I move through to Ward 4. There is a group of people staring at an old television like it holds some secret to salvation that would otherwise evaporate like the roll-up smoke and suffocate under the softly-softly footsteps of the zombie-dancer as they shuffle up and down the corridor, up and down the corridor. I had found the Empire of the Lost, that final frontier at which all sense melts away to be replaced by a kind of mesmeric rhythm that plays out the drumbeat of lives that only semi-exist. There is a clock on one of the walls. I notice that it has stopped. Time frozen. It is the singularity where all laws of physics break down. It is the edge of a black hole that never changes, that forms out of static eternity the ultimate dirge to forgetting. Life and the universe become the roll-up on the lip, a sagging existence that knows only the inevitability of death.

I go into the television room. A nurse takes me over to someone I know I recognize. Someone I knew, once. *Mary, you have a visitor.*

Mary looks up. Her bright red hair has turned into a form of brown and appears greasy. She is clothed in a nightie covered in coffee stains and an old dressing gown which has been burned with countless cigarettes. She has a roll-up in her mouth which she puffs at compulsively. Her hands and legs are shaking. Constant up and down movements, *that is what I remember most.* Her fingers shake as she draws on her roll-up. Her feet are constantly moving up and down, up and down. She looks at me, her gaze empty, like someone has stolen her, her life, her vitality, and replaced it with an emptiness so pure that it might be the depths of space. Her gaze fixes on me for about five minutes without her saying anything. I move to touch her but her arm seems frozen in its own moment. No response, just that cold black emptiness that fills the space between us and subsumes it. Her gaze doesn't change. Fixed. The event horizon, a beginning without an end, and an end without beginning ...

A single tear runs down her face.

I decided that I was going to be everything they did not want me to be.

The   Ghosts

We   Form

Of   Our   Lives

Sing

Their   Hymns

As   Testament

To   The   Lost

23

My broken angel, I dream of you still, I
Move through the memories that they stole from us, we
Motion through the image of the field of barley and running
wild, we
Scatter ourselves before the sun that gave birth to the moment
of our dawning, we
Move through each heartbeat that we shared and I see you
there still, your
Red hair trapping the light and shimmering in a wondrous
ode to the freedom that was, we
Move through each distance like the song of a star that is
borne at the edge of the universe which we created when, we
Moved through the moon-splattered ponds and dipped our
feet into the water where, we
Exalted ourselves on the interface of our beginning, there

Is no greater desolation than the loss of hope, my
Tears fall down your face as we cling to the last remnant of
being.

24

I go back to the airport, back to Manchester, back to university. I feel a kind of numbness, like my reality has been kind of sucked from me, like I am in some kind of vacuum chamber that pulls me and pushes me at the same time. I want to cry, but the tears won't come.

I decide that I am going to become everything they didn't want me to be.

On my way back to college I buy a bottle of Scottish Malt Whiskey. It was kind of expensive but I thought I would have a wake. A wake for life and dreams. A wake for the universe. I go into my room, lock the door and put on a tape, *Sonic Youth,* something angry. I tear up my lecture notes and my textbooks, light a cigarette and open the bottle. I find a glass and pour out a shot. Then another shot, then another. I feel like I am slipping away from myself. The sensation is strangely comforting. The whiskey tastes good. It eases down my throat like relief. The tape finishes and I put on another, *The Pixies, Where is my mind?* Good question. I drink another shot. Then

I start laughing and crying at the same time. Uncontrollably. I remember dancing at Mr O'Connor's gate and the single tear down the face. I shout at life and its malice and take another shot. In about an hour, I have the bottle finished and am lying semi-comatose on the bed …

The next morning I feel awful. My hands are shaking and I feel the need to get sick. I look at my watch, 11am. I look at my torn notes and books. I look at the tape recorder, the tapes, the kettle, the jar of coffee, the empty bottle of Scottish Malt Whiskey. I gather some clothes together and stuff them into a case. I put what remains of my money in my pocket. I decide to go to London.

So, I get on the train. I watch the life I have lived for the last few months slip away like it was only an ephemeral reality that one imagined when one was drunk. I have a bottle of cheap wine on me and conceal it in a brown paper bag like the homeless man in Cork City had done with his vodka. I take a swig from time to time whilst compulsively smoking cigarette after cigarette. The train travels through life like its own imagination, passing through each reality, one to the next, a process of continuing dreaming that moves through its own undecipherable logic. I am hungry and manage to find half a sandwich in my coat pocket (how it got there I don't know). I eat it like I haven't eaten for weeks. I take another swig of wine and put my head back against the seat. Everything seems to be going round and round, a carousel of pain, a pain that splits like migraine and sublimates into reality like the spirit of a lost life that calls through the wind and the barley like a memory to those Aboriginal songs through which creation came to be ...

Existence

Is   Nothing

But   Its   Own

Illusion

25

I arrive at King's Cross feeling awful. I stagger off the train and go to a coffee shop and order a double expresso and then another, which I drink quickly. I am not sure where to go. I go to a youth hostel and book myself in for the night. I fall asleep early.

I get up, looking around me just to make sure that everything is real. I decide to buy a paper and look for a house share, and possibly some kind of work. I notice that a restaurant is looking for someone to do wash up, and I decide to apply.

The manager notes my accent and asks me why I want a job like this. I decide to be honest, *Because I have nothing left.* He says that I appear to be both honest and young and strong, and that he would take me on.

I start at 9.30pm and work until past 1am. I don't mind. The physical labour keeps my mind off things and the little bit of money is useful. I spend the days walking. Walking everywhere. Sometimes I sit in a coffee shop. Sometimes I buy whiskey, or wine, and sit on park benches. Sometimes I find a quiet place, like a church, and think of Mary, and cry silently.

I find the possibility of a house share. I call them up and they agree to meet me. They live in a house in East London that is relatively accessible to the restaurant where I work. A young lad with shortish hair opens the door. He has a broad east London accent and invites me in. There are pictures of West Ham United everywhere, as well as a St George's Cross, and one of those flags from the American South. There are overflowing ashtrays, beer cans, and empty takeaway pizza boxes everywhere.

I decide to be everything they don't want me to be …

I explain that my name is John and that I am kind of homeless. They note my accent but don't appear to be overly hostile. They introduce themselves as Mike, Bill and Tom. They ask me what I think of West Ham United. I tell them that I don't really know. They laugh and tell me that they will take me to a match on Saturday (I have the evening off work), and that I am welcome to stay. They offer me a beer, and a smoke, which I gratefully accept. I move from the youth hostel and settle in. I have a small bedroom at the top. There is a large poster relating to West Ham United over the bed.

Beginnings

And

Endings

Jostle

For

Position

98

26

The match is West Ham vs Chelsea. We travel by tube to Upton Park, swigging beers and shouting abuse at anyone we might suspect to be a Chelsea fan. A group of Chelsea fans start singing *Fuck 'em all! Fuck 'em all! United, West Ham and Liverpool! Because we are the Chelsea and we are the best! We are the Chelsea so fuck all the rest!* Mike shouts back, *Chelsea rent boys! Chelsea rent boys!* One of the Chelsea fans takes a swing at Mike. I feel a bit nervous. Bill says that this is all part of the fun and it gets better after the match. Then one has a real fight! Mike fends off the Chelsea fan and Tom takes a swing at him. The Chelsea fan falls over and drops his beer. Mike says, *I hate Chelsea! I am not sure why*. I can't really figure out what the Chelsea fans did to him apart from following another team. But there is something electrifying about it. The danger of the situation gives me a spark of something, I don't know what, but something. Like it reflects all the anger inside me. I can concentrate all the anger on Chelsea Football Club. That concentration gives my anger a focus. I can see its meaning in the greasy burgers on sale at the ground, in the cans of superstrength lager, the cups of Thames mud coffee …

There is an enormous crowd of people. Some waving West Ham banners and dressed in West Ham scarves, some waving Chelsea banners and dressed in Chelsea scarves. The volatile nature invigorates me, like I exist hand-in-hand with the incipient violence, the sense of testosterone aggression … I imagine the Chelsea fans to be representing my parents, the people that took Mary and Finn away, every grievance, through school, through not fitting in … The violence forms a meaning, a description, something one can hold in one's hands and sense as real … We enter the stadium. The Chelsea fans have their own area. The teams come onto the pitch and there is a roar. The roar echoes like all my pain, painting it on the stands, on the pitch, on the Chelsea fans. A reason to hate? Ultimately there is no reason to hate, so we manufacture a reason. We shout at the Chelsea fans. And they shout at us. And we communicate in this way, the aggression, the sense of meaninglessness that needs to find its resolution through the crowds …

One of the West Ham players goes down in the box. The crowd (and some of the West Ham players) scream for a penalty, but the referee is not interested and waves play on. There erupts an enormous cry of *The referee's a wanker!* All seems focused on the man, with the whistle in the middle of the field, made smaller and smaller through the repeated cry of *The referee's a wanker!* I form of everything that has gone wrong in my life and direct it onto the figure on the pitch. I shout as loud as I can, *The referee's a wanker! THE REFEREE'S A WANKER!* Something seems resolved, I don't know what exactly, but something. The referee becomes my parents, the teachers at my school, *The referee's a wanker!* The referee becomes my job in the restaurant, *The referee's a wanker!* The referee becomes the dinner parties and a million conversations going only where they've been before, *The referee's a wanker!* The referee becomes the taking away of the only person I have ever really loved, *The referee's a wanker …*

West Ham scores and there is exultation. I feel the achievement of the goal as being part of me, even though I have had little practical involvement in the scoring of it. I begin to feel the real attraction of football. One is part of something, and when that something wins, we win. The goal is as much of us as it is of the player who scored it. Everyone around me seems to throw their arms around me as if I am somehow responsible. And I throw my arms around someone next to me, someone covered with tattoos who periodically sings *God Save the Queen* It is the first time I have met someone like this. He has a shaved head and is wearing Docker boots. He is the epitome of aggression, the epitome of *my aggression.* I feel a strange bond with him, a man who has dedicated his life to hatred.

101

I wonder why he has become like that. What happened to him? What has he experienced? He starts waving a St George's Cross. Something about that man and about England, becoming part of each other in a search for a superiority that has evaporated in history, seeking a means to be better, better than what? Something inside me wants to ask if he would like to meet for a drink. Not because we have much in common. Or perhaps because we have everything in common … Forming translations out of being lost, and found. Attempting to resurrect some concept of empire out of empty plastic glasses and botulism burgers, through the fact of the referee being a wanker … An image of a past that finds its justification in hatred for the referee, the scoring of the goal. An image of a past that sprays itself like graffiti on the walls of our senselessness. An empire of the senseless born out of empire's demise *God save our gracious Queen. God save the Queen …*

The   Distance

Of   History

Glimpses

Its   Image

In   Its   Mirage

27

It is nearly full time and West Ham are one up. Then there is a contentious incident in the box where a Chelsea player might have had claims for a penalty. The whole ground is poised in silence. One could, as the cliche goes, have cut the atmosphere with a knife. Tens of thousands of people watch the referee like he holds the meaning of the entire universe in his whistle. He moves. Slowly. He gives the penalty. Chelsea scores. The shout of, *The referee's a wanker!* rises up in the air like a sacrifice to the hidden anger that exists in all of us. The West Ham supporters start ripping up the seats in the stadium and throwing them onto the ground. The match is over. The players leave the field and fans from both sides flood onto the pitch. Mike shouts *Chelsea rent boys!* at a group of Chelsea fans in one corner. They congregate around him and started punching him, over and over. I feel the need to defend my new housemate and start lashing out at the Chelsea fans who are hitting him with part of one of the seats that has been ripped out of the stands. I have never really been in a fight before, but again I feel the translation, the sense that somehow the match, the shouting, the violence, echoes my life and is in some way part of me ... I grab one of the Chelsea fans by his coat and swing him to the ground. Another of them grabs me but I manage to defend myself adequately. At this point Mike gets back on his feet and kicks at the Chelsea fan that I have knocked over. Blood starts pouring out of his nose. I feel somewhere inside that I should try to stop it, but another part compels me to carry on. I start to kick the Chelsea fan also, finding expression in the aggression, finding a meaning that has been lost since the time when they took Mary away ... I feel strangely alive, like I belong to something, like I have found a resolution to all the pain and the meaninglessness. I have an image of Mother peeling the potatoes and kick out at that. I have an image of Father and his cricket and whiskey and kick out at that. I have an image of a thousand million things that I am angry with. I have an image of *God save the Queen* and kick out at that. Forms of a dysfunction. Of a dysfunction that forms of an ultimate meaning rather than the formulae through which we define ourselves, through which we define others, through which one weaves the fabric of our lives into the cloth of our meaninglessness. And then we take the cloth and wrap it around ourselves. We become invisible. And through that invisibility we come to see everything ... because no one can see us ... no one can judge us ... no one can contradict us.

We emerge out of the ultimate knowledge through refuting all knowledge. We focus and we slip away. We form so that no one can ever touch us again. No one can hurt us again. And as we kick out, we form to connect. Because so much of life seems to be about violence. We have no reason to hate the Chelsea fans, except for the fact of there being no reason to hate them. We hurt someone that we don't know because hurting them gives us reason. And when asked why, we respond, *But you don't know him, so why should you care? Did you care about the genocides of history? Did you rush to join Amnesty International when you read about humanity's pain in the newspaper?* It is easy to judge. So, I kick a man. And he might spend a couple of hours in Accident and Emergency. But we turn away when there is the fear that one might be obliged to do something about the world. One focuses on West Ham and Chelsea. In the meantime, Nestlé sells baby formula to the developing world with the propaganda that it will make African babies healthy, like babies in the developed world. And the mothers buy the stuff and stop breast feeding. And then they can no longer afford it. Or they are forced to mix it with cholera infected water. And the breast milk dries up. And the babies starve. And Nestlé is well aware of this. Philip Morris sells cigarettes cheap to the developing world in order to get people addicted. And then they raise the price. And yet we focus on West Ham and Chelsea. I kick a man

I do not know. But I have become part of something and elect to defend that thing. I am not condoning violence. But somehow, in this little instance, violence has its own song ...

We move and dance to the tune of, *The referee's a wanker!*

Images   Find

Their   Own   Futility

Through   The   Rocks

Out   Of   Which

They   Are   Carved

28

I find Bill, Mike and Tom in the mêlée and we decide to make our way home. Bill asks me, *What did you think?* I say that I enjoyed it and would like to go with them again. Before getting home, we decide to go for a few beers. We go to this pub. I have never been there before. It is an old pub. 19th Century. Possibly older. There are a group of old men at the bar, drinking whiskey, and a somewhat scratchy blues tape on in the background. I have a minor injury on my hand but nothing serious. I order a pint of Carlsberg and a whiskey chaser. My new friends order a pint each and we sit down. We talk about the match, the goal, the penalty … And we talk about the fight. Mike says, *Our posh friend is definitely West Ham. It's in his blood. You should have seen him get stuck in.* The three put their arms around me and say, *We're proud of you, mate. Next Saturday we'll take you to Millwall. Now there's a fight …* I feel a belonging like I've never felt before. Like I am part of something. Like I have a name, an identity *West Ham United.*

We have another drink, and then another. I look at the old men at the bar, their silent dreams clinking in the ice in their whiskey glasses as they order another shot. I try and imagine their histories. Some of them look old enough to be veterans of World War II. I imagine them at Dunkirk, watching the arms of fallen comrades drift in the sea water like a dirge to all the memories that we lose. I imagine them with a gun, knowing that they will have to shoot men in order to survive. I imagine them being part of Bomber Harris' squadron and the bombing of Dresden. Angels of death fighting for a better world … or maybe fighting because fighting becomes all that they understand. I look at the rheumy eyes and the sadness that sticks to one like the car pollution on Marylebone road. I imagine peace and violence coming together, like whiskey on ice, each one the justification of the other. I imagine them coming back from war to a society that they have ceased to understand *I have seen too much* … I imagine a search for redemption that echoes through the dark halls of fame that history has created for us. The subtle movements through which we drift through life, finding resolution in ashtrays and cigarette butts *I spit out the butt ends of my days and ways* … We seem to sway together in some intoxicated dance that reverberates to the tune of *The referee's a wanker!* Dunkirk. Everything. We seek to explain so much but ultimately the universe is inexplicable. They say that in quantum mechanics a particle can communicate with another instantaneously (they call this *entanglement*). No history, no passing of time … Existence forms of a crystal that shimmers eternally before becoming lost in its own light. I am, and you are. You are, and I am. And we are together in this tiny chink of spacetime that we call our lives. And as you travel relative to me, you travel a little bit into my future. And every time we see a star, we see it as it was a million years ago. We describe histories as a relationship between moments. The moments create themselves and then divide into their own fractions before spiralling off into memories of their own particular nothingness, a thousand paintings in the portrait gallery of ages, *This is you, this is me, this is us.* And we move through our distance and our coming together … The old men congeal in their silence. They are form out of their own particular autobiography with each sip of whiskey. I feel a strange form of empathy. Like we created the universe together through our memories, me, the old men, the particles of our life coming together in some mystic fusion of abstraction that speaks through the multiple lives that we live. *I am West Ham. I have become West Ham because I needed something to be. We fear being nothing because the nothingness negates us. So, we are West Ham. And West Ham gives us its reason.* The blues tape ends and we float as if levitating in the silence, the silence that is only broken through the chink of whiskey on ice. The silence that becomes everything and nothing at the same time …

Moments

Drift

Through

The   Silence

Of   Their   Realities

29

I imagine you through the water that rushes through our lives, like the

Beginning of a dream that describes the funeral march of its ending

I hold your hand through the distance, the blood-red moon calls to us

I move through the dances and the love songs that scatter themselves at the feet of our being, I

Move through the slow whisper through which you repeated each story in my ear, I

Am through the forests that grew at our birthing and the Dawn chorus birds of our awakening, I

Capture your image in the freeze-frame of my memory, everything I was and everything I am now, echoes in movements that

Splinter their sacrifices on the altars of our sensing, I

Hold your hand and drift through the universe that I am now, I
Feel the tears on your cheek as a testament to our loss.

30

Saturday and Millwall. We decide to have a few preparatory pints and crowd into a pub full of fellow West Ham supporters. We start to sing. The songs become more incoherent with each pint, with each testimony to the thrill of aggression ... We go to Blackfriars and then catch a two-carriage train to the Millwall ground known as The Den. There are Millwall supporters also. These seem even more aggressive than the Chelsea fans and their aggression courses through my body like some kind of rush that I find hard to define. I feel alive in the atmosphere of danger, in the sense that one exists on the edge of something that both threatens you and calls to you at the same time ...

We get to the ground. There are groups of both West Ham and Millwall supporters exchanging insults. One of the Millwall fans strikes at one of ours with a broken bottle and blood pours down his face as he falls over. Some of the other West Ham supporters rush to his aid and a random fight breaks out, fists, knives, broken bottles. It seemed like a form of reality that we ignore and yet calls to us. I think of the old men at the pub, each one of them drinking a swansong to their own lives and difficulties, the violence buried inside, the echo of living through danger and fear and then resolving it through the eternal search for oblivion … We exist in many forms. And we form so as to compensate for our histories, marking time, crossing off each day on the calendar of our lives like a funeral. I move through a hundred movements in one, drifting through …

We enter the ground. *The referee's a wanker!* That eternal cry towards ultimate meaning, ultimate absurdity, both. We raise our hands in a salute to the cacophony of aggression that moves through us like blood, that becomes the life force of all that we are through its own elegy … The Millwall supporters begin ripping up the stadium at the beginning of the second half. The cacophony reaches its ultimate height. People run onto the pitch throwing the remainders of the chairs, bottles, bricks, anything that can be found. It appears that the Millwall supporters are even attacking each other, though in the surge of fists and bodies it is difficult to tell.

Then the police come. The mounted police enter the ground and force both the Millwall supporters and the West Ham supporters back. The supporters rush for the exit and pour out onto the street like some post-apocalyptic cry towards the nothingness that exists as the tribute to our meaning. The Millwall supporters and the West Ham supporters end up facing each other across the road. The police sit on their horses, waiting nervously. A West Ham supporter cries *Millwall scum!* and a Millwall supporter grabs a brick and throws it hard at him. It glances off his head and he falls over. Then a West Ham supporter picks up a broken bottle and runs at a group of Millwall supporters at the corner of the road. The Millwall supporters intercept him and he is pushed to the ground. I am unable to see what happens to him. Then a West Ham supporter lobs a Molotov cocktail at the group of Millwall supporters and sets the clothes of one of them alight. One of the Millwall supporters sets fire to a car. The police try to intervene but they are well outnumbered. The only way out of the place is a narrow path that leads to the station at which the train back to Blackfriars stands, but the place is packed with people, and the train only has two carriages, and only leaves every 40 minutes. I am not sure if I will live or die. The feeling scares and excites me at the same time. I am approached by a Millwall supporter and I hit him, I don't know why, but it seemed appropriate, like it is what's called for under the circumstances, like I have to be *West Ham* and the definition of *West Ham* is hating everything that is not West Ham. I look at my hand, there is blood, I don't know whether it is mine or his. Tom and Bill are with me. Mike is somewhere else, likely in the street at the epicentre of the violence. Mike is the most aggressive of our little group. We stay like that for at least two hours. Both Millwall and West Ham have declared war against the whole area, cars alight and windows smashed. Groups run against each other. Some have weapons such as knives. Others brandish bricks, Molotov cocktails, or bits of wood from the smashed stadium seats.

I look at myself and have never felt so near death, never so alive, than at any other part of my life

We Paint

The Portrait

Of Our Ultimate Reasons

Through

The Ever-turning Circles

Of Our Desperation

31

And so this is life. I work in the restaurant in the week and go to football every Saturday. The thought of the football manages to compensate for the routine of my work. In a way, I actually enjoy the meaninglessness of the work, it fits into something, I do not know exactly what. Sometimes I go to the pub that Mike, Bill and Tom took me to after the Chelsea match. I feel a kind of strange attraction to the place. I buy pints and whiskey chasers, spending most of my wages. I sit at the bar with the old men. I want to communicate with them, to hear their stories and their pain, to move through their universes a bit ... but they are too engrossed in their whiskey and their silent pain to notice me. The same blues tape plays Muddy Waters, I think, I am not sure. I sit there until closing time in my silent communication with the world. I imagine the old men and I living in a sort of astral plane connection through which our lives have become inextricably bound through the silence that flows through us and etches its own silent communication. I move through myself over and over, connecting with some ephemeral dream of Mary by the lake, her red hair glinting in the sun, the love and then the pain that brought me here. I motion through myself, calling to some former life in the froth of my Carlsberg and in the golden glow my whiskey makes in the lights above the bar.

The loneliness of the place calls me more and more. I begin missing days at work and going to the pub as soon as it opens, waiting at the door for the barmaid to open it. I order a pint and a chaser, and sit at what has become my favourite seat at the bar, looking at the old men with their whiskeys …

I feel that the whole universe exists in this pub. The rheumy-eyed old men are a kind of physical description of the emptiness of space and of the distances that history forms as we move through the quick, quick slow journeys that define us. I am one with you, and yet eternally separated from you. We hold hands together and spiral through the distances that separate us. You form to be me but only I can be me, even if I ultimately want to be you. We seek the meaning of humanity, so many of us, and yet also the loneliness that seeps through our dreams like whiskey, that glints through its own dirge to the forming of our ending … We move towards company, and find that company refutes us. And then we come to refute it, and order another whiskey. And each image moves through us, repeating over and over the mantra of our despair. Zen in the whiskey glass, hymns to the absurd rising up with our cigarette smoke as we draw in deeply another breath towards our forgetting. We move through the dreams of youth, Mary's hair glinting in the sun, before we form an elegy to joy vanquished and have another glass ... We find ourselves in those tiny little movements we make; the lifting of the glass to one's lips, taking a sip, and then putting it down again. We count these moments on the abacus of our lives. My life has become football, and the pub, the pub that calls to me when I awake in the morning and sings its lullaby to me as I go to sleep. We move through different spaces; I can be West Ham or I can be the man in the pub who finds his own particular prayer in the whiskey and the ice. I think of Mary, my last image of her, the single tear on her cheek as she stared vacantly with her hands constantly moving, constantly moving. I saw my new addiction to West Ham as a kind of funeral for her, and the pub as her wake. We seek to make sense and yet sense eludes us becoming its own phantom and drifting through the window, we try to catch it, but as soon as we feel near to it, we find that it is gone ...

Echoes

Through

The   Dreams

That   Steal

Our   Sleep

Like

Thieves

32

I find a public telephone box and call the hospital where I last saw Mary. There is a voice at the other end, precise in its distance, that asks me if I am a family friend. I reply, *Kinda, yes.*

The voice at the other end says, *I am sorry to tell you this ...* My heart feels like it is going to collapse. *Mary passed away last week.*

How?

She took her own life ...

I feel that I am in slow motion and speeding up at the same time. My head is racing. I feel sweaty, hot and cold at the same time. I drop the receiver. It dangles there like an elegy to a thousand dead memories ...

Distance

Moves

Through   The   Reality

Of   Its   Own

Ghost

33

Memories splinter into a thousand pieces,

I am and I am not

The distance that catches us between a million dreams that

scatter their sparks toward the night sky

I am

I am not

My definition floats through the moon and cries its

desperation

Ashes form through the interface

I see each movement that we made painted on the sky

I drift through and in myself, a

Howling wolf's testimony to the universal pain that made itself

through the swansong of our being.

34

I go to the night pub. The old men are still there, their silent rituals painted through the distance and caught in the melancholy of the blues tape. I order a Carlsberg and a whiskey chaser, I down the whiskey quickly and feel a little light headed. I try and form a reality here, the meaning behind the glint in the ice and all the ghosts it sings its hymns towards. Existing is the hardest thing ... I watch my own hand lifting the glass, toasting some forgotten God that moves through the blues tape and the old men. I try and imagine what they have seen in life. I imagine them to be war veterans again. What death has brought them here? I imagine Dunkirk and the dead arms moving with the sea. I want to cry but I don't know how to ... I feel caught in this little piece of space time, the closeness and the distance that describes each one of us and our intersection through the history through which we have come to be. I imagine, if they are war veterans, have they seen death? Is the whiskey some form of sacrifice to Isis? I don't know. I feel like I know everything about them and yet nothing at all. I want to reach out and touch them. Why?

Because they seem real. More real than reality. I try to form through my memories what their memories might have been. Flying over Dresden and destroying it and then spending the rest of one's life trying to justify ... what? That death exists? I imagine again them flying through the night in their bomber planes, angels of death, angels of life. And I imagine the Dresden population looking at the airborne apocalypse with their own questions, their own reality. I imagine what it must be like to see a dead person ... The old men move through their connection with some forgotten pain that carves itself upon a thousand headstones. How many lost friends? Family? The whiskey forms part of their coming-to-be, I exist ... I exist because I am no longer capable of existing. One of the old men's eyes are red. Red from the whiskey? Or red from a million silent tears that scattered themselves through Dunkirk, Dresden ... I find I desperately want to know his name. And yet I don't ask him because the distance between us seems so real, compulsively real. And in that reality is some type of salvation, a salvation I have searched for since I came to London. The endless dance of pain ... Reaching out, I touch the bar and motion to the girl behind it (who knows me quite well by now) for another pint and another chaser, which she duly provides. I light a cigarette and inhale deeply ... The smoke exists like some form of incense to the forgotten God that lurks through the whiskey bottles and stuff, describing his universe through me, through all of us in the pub, seeking to form of some answer to … what? That pain exists? That pain is real? That we would not know the light if it wasn't for the darkness? I feel a thousand questions and the desperate search for answers. I turn to one of the old men and ask him whether he fought in World War II and what was it like. He turns to me slowly and says nothing, just watches me with those red, rheumy eyes. He seems more real, more completely real, than the universe itself, the whole of creation caught in the silent look and the bringing of the glass to his lips, the swallowing … I move through my distance, feeling more lonely and yet more connected than words can ever express. I feel the world revolve beneath me in its endless Shiva's dance of love and pain, each destruction sparking off its own creativity. We are two systems, the light and the dark. And we move through these systems like some quantum particle seeking the reality of its potential to exist. We are, we are not. We float through a thousand Easters, crucifixions, and new life. And we exist like this, between the form of light and dark, between the waking hours and the dreams that stalk us in the middle of the night. The pub is an intersection. It is where the two meet and ply their realities against the backdrop of the whiskey and the silent old men. I imagine a Big Bang occurring behind the bottles of whiskey, an extreme creative moment that spirals through each minute we sit there, catching us in the vortex of its own pain, its own longing … I light another cigarette and the smoke catches me at the back of the throat. And brings me out of my reverie for a bit. I imagine Shiva dancing on the bar, through the whiskey glasses and the ashtrays, calling us to salvation, oblivion, both. I feel that I have died today. And yet I also feel that I have lived more than I have ever lived. Why? Because there seems to be some form of resolution, because I form of my Easter … resurrecting through the pain that catches us like cigarette smoke, the distant longing that paints itself upon the windows, defines its art through the ashtrays, the blues tape, the silent song of the desperate.

I left the pub and cried, cried like I have never cried before.

Images   Form

Of   Their   Own   Reality

When   They   Learn   How   To   Die

35

Echoes of the night hold my hand …

I dance through the beginning and the end of things

Painting through each Yin and Yang the processes through
which I give birth to myself and then die

I float through the halls of fame that define the processes of
our history

I move through the Silence that calls us through to celebrate its
own particular oblivion

I am

I am the movement on the lake surface created by the stone
thrown into the water

I am the movement of the trees and the wind whispering in
the leaves

I am a thousand things, drifting through the autumn to the
winter of my existence

I am the crunch of the frost beneath feet as I walk on a winter
morning

I catch myself through the light and then a black hole, through
the images of each death I imagine in the form of my crying,
I move through the silent slipstream where the silver shimmer
of the moonlight paints its own graffiti on the walls of our
forgetting
I drink to life
I drink to death
Both

36

The pub is shut, but I don't feel like going home quite yet. I decide to go to a nightclub. I don't know why, I never particularly liked them, but maybe I don't feel resolved quite yet …

I go to the door and pay the man my entrance. There seems to be some sort of dance music on. The place is crowded, a swirl of people moving through some manic-depressive delirium of forgetting. I decide to have a drink. I order an extremely expensive pint of Heineken and then dance. Maybe the rhythm will bring some type of connection, I don't know. So I enter the delirium and move through the pain that crashes on one's awareness like the strobe lights, moving and moving, twirling through some ritual to forgetting that shatters across my brain like glass … I am, I am not. The music seems to take over, to enter me and move me through its own formations, the bodies and the music, some sort of car crash moment that catches itself around me and sweeps me through to its own unreality … I move through a thousand universes, tripping between the supernovae and the black holes that they become. I feel like I am moving through past and future, through some Feynman diagram of a quasi-existence through which time is symmetrical, forwards and backwards, it doesn't matter, the equations remain the same. I am a particle crashing into a million other particles and becoming each one before I fade into the distance of a longing through which I see Mary by the lake, her red hair glimmering, through which I see West Ham United, a thousand realities each one competing with the other for my attention. I crash through some CERN Geneva experiment through which I hold hands with Shiva and spin through the birth of the universe and my own dying, the dying that I feel inside, the dying that spins through the dance music ... I am at a funeral. My funeral. And maybe I will come back from the dead. Maybe not. I don't know, I can't tell ... Shiva calls me through the Milky Way and the sparkle of the stars that invites us to become, to forget, both. The intoxicating movement through which my history emerges out of its own dark hall of fame, the old men, Mary, West Ham ... floating above me and beyond me, through me and in me, like a final moment when existence reveals its own meaning in the dance of Shiva through the stars, the hand that reaches to me and tells me to become, to negate ...

I feel tired from the dancing and sit down with another pint. A young lad approaches me, he has a t-shirt, and a bandanna, and a bright white smile that seemed to exude confidence. He asks me if I am enjoying myself, *Well, sort of.* He tells me that he can help me enjoy myself more. I ask him *How?* He opens his hand and reveals some small blue tablets. *Want some?* I take the tablets and swallow them down with my drink. He gives me a scrap of paper and introduces himself as Nick *You want more, call this number.* I put the paper in my pocket …

Things swirl around me. The lights blend into one and the music becomes a cacophony of sound that calls, calls … I spin around and exist. I am my own supernova, I am my own black hole. Feelings numb as the pulse of the dance floor becomes ever more prevalent, a beating heart that enters my heart, that tells me of the thousands of things I could be, that wraps its forgetting like some sort of healing blanket that shimmers with the rhythm. I move through a thousand ages, gripping hold of myself as I move through the slipstream through which my existence floats from me and merges with the strobe lighting, with the forgetting. I move through the ghosts that circle around me, each one calling to me, each one becoming me as I oscillate wildly through a form of existence that fabricates its own mythology through the strobe lighting, that creates of one a momentary hero that forms through the ultimate conquering … Shiva whispers through the music and calls me to spin round Jupiter, the starlight sparkling through Mary's hair as she sits by the lake laughing … A thousand moments collide and create something new, something old, the birth of something so ancient that it inscribes its name through the beginning of time … Shiva calls me to eternity and I touch it with my fingers, the shimmering light that flows through, ever present but uncacheable, ever moving through the processes through which time reaches out and gives birth to itself, moving through the Feynman diagram in which I move as one particle before colliding with another and becoming something else. Life is a flux. Life calls in the random shake of the dice through which we were born and through which we die. Shiva calls through the beginning of the whole of things, inviting me to take part, to spin in the dance in which all was created, to join with the light that sneaks under the door we tried to close. Shiva hovers above the strobe lighting, expanding, becoming ever more real as the nightclub, the dancers, shrink into the form of their own nothingness. I levitate and float around the ceiling somewhere, catching the music like language, becoming its song, my bones vibrate in a dance of their own, moving through the moment. Shiva moves through the life and the afterlife, catching Heaven within his dance, his hands moving through a thousand tapestries, existing and moving through closeness and distance, watching the universe give birth to itself through a primordial song that twists its energy round the processes of its singing. The probabilities of life move through the story of a star that died a million years ago and then gave birth to itself, motioning and existing. Shiva throws the dice and the game begins. The game of life. Death. Both. I move through some Riemann sphere of abstraction, reality stating that it is real only because it is not real. What is real? We search all of our lives. And we fail to find it. We move through journeys without either beginnings or endings. Eternity is every moment that has ever existed. Eternity is a single moment that stretches itself through the universal fabric, making the gravity waves in and around us, calling some quantum call of randomness that paints its own portrait and then scatters it between the stars. Echoes and being. Echoes and being. And which is real? The echoes because they call to us? Or the being because it doesn't exist? And maybe the ultimate form of existence is when one ceases to exist. When our lives become condensed in some other form. When we transcend. When we relinquish all but that moment. That moment could be anything. It could be Mother peeling the potatoes. It could be Mary laughing by the lake. We choose. And we are chosen. It is through choosing that we become chosen. And when we are chosen we make sense, because ultimately, sense doesn't exist. And we catch that little splinter of light in our hand that was created in every beginning that was begun. Every end that was ended.

Existence

Curls

Its   Fingers

Upon

Our   Time

Like   The   Ghosts

That   Stalk

The   Corridors

Of   Our   Being

37

Mike, Bill and Tom invite me to a meeting. *The speaker's good. You'll enjoy it!* We catch the Tube to Stockwell and enter a pub. The pub looks rough. There is a stage, behind which is draped a Union Jack. Nearly everyone has shaved heads. I become a little self-conscious about my longish hair. There is an aggression that you can touch, it feels sticky, cloying. Many of the men also have Union Jacks on their t-shirts. They are wearing heavy boots.

The speaker gets on the stage. *We are here to talk about England. In some circles, it is unfashionable, the wrong thing to do. But we are here because we care about England, what it is, what it should be, and what it risks becoming.* I get myself a pint.

The men with the shaved heads look rapt and nod their heads muttering, *Here here.* The man continues. *Now the country is full of immigrants. They are not English, but they are taking us over. Pakis ...* I feel myself floating somewhere between my pint and the stage, the men nodding their heads and muttering *Here here.* I find it hard to focus. *Pakis, who come over here and are given social housing when the English THE REAL ENGLISH have to do without. Who run shops and charge the English THE REAL ENGLISH a fortune. Who bring their religion ...* I am paying attention and not paying attention at the same time. *They come over here and charge us what they like. When they should be paying us ...* I feel distance, a disconnect. *We are not allowed to fly our flag because some feel that it is not politically correct. We are not allowed to sing God Save the Queen.* I think of several times when I have heard people singing *God Save the Queen* without anyone trying to stop them. *Their children take our school places, and the schools have to teach their religion ...* I am somewhere between Jupiter and Mars. *They take jobs from the English THE REAL ENGLISH ...*

The talk lasts for about an hour and a half. Afterwards, we all go into the main body of the pub for a pint. Tom asks me what I think. I don't say much. I just order another pint and sit down. We stay for a good three hours and we are all somewhat drunk. The aggression builds. We sing *God Save the Queen* and raise our hands. The other people at the pub look on in a mixture of what I think is both fear and curiosity. The singing gets more intense. I feel an intense claustrophobia, as if I can't really breathe. I think, *When I get out of here, I will call Nick and get some more of those pills.* My head feels as if it is aching,

139

my hands shake. I think that this is some form of withdrawal from the pills, or maybe just the atmosphere in the pub, maybe both, I am not sure. But my head feels swimmy and I find myself clinging to the bottom of my chair in fear of falling over. My breathing becomes erratic, I feel sick …

On leaving the pub, Mike seems particularly aggressive. He gives me a knife and invites me to *Teach those Pakis a lesson*. We walk into a small off license, and Mike demands that the shop owner gives him a whiskey. The shop owner says *That will be twenty pounds*. Mike's face goes red … I can feel incipient danger creeping through the shop, under the display cases, under the door, around the cash till … Mike says, *You what?* The shop owner repeats his demand. Mike starts shouting, and waving his knife about. The shop owner tells him to take the whiskey and to leave him alone. Mike then smashes the beer fridge and kicks the cans all over the place. The shop owner is definitely frightened now. Mike starts shouting *You fucking Pakis, expect me to pay? You should be paying us … You come into our country … Fucking stinks of curry in here. Fucking stinks of the stuff …* He then grabs the shop owner, throws him to the floor and starts kicking him. Bill and Tom join in. I try to reason with them but there are three of them and one of me, and I feel sick. We leave the shop with the shop owner lying on the floor, bleeding. I say, *I am going for a walk*.

I am not sure where I am going. The night lamps glisten. The mist forms halos around them like forgotten dreams. I have about thirty pounds in my pocket. I go to a public telephone and ring Nick. He agrees to meet me. I buy some more of the pills and wash them down with some cheap vodka that I buy from a corner shop (not unlike the one that Mike trashed). I feel more normal. I sit on a shop doorway and try to think. The world seems ephemeral, like it is floating somewhere between its reality and its dreaming. I breathe in, out, in, out. *God Save the Queen* seems to echo in the background. At least my hands have stopped shaking. I feel tired, but unable to go to sleep. The night is cold and I wrap my arms around myself and shiver. The pills begin to take effect and my mind is floating somewhere between the mist and the glow of the street lamps. Night people move to-and-fro in their own routines, their own songs. I float somewhere in deep space, drifting through spacetime, feeling it embrace me with its gravity. I move through the thousand possibilities of what is, what should have been. My eyes track the night people. I wonder where they are all going *where I am going.* I find a public ash tray and collect a few butts, reach into my pocket for a lighter and light one of them up. I inhale deeply, my head is spinning. I lean against the shop doorway and try to control my breathing, in, out, in, out. I fall into an uncomfortable sleep, still hearing *God Save the Queen* reverberating round my head, it seems to have got inside the whole of me … I remember the shop owner on the floor. I try to tell someone to call an ambulance to see if he is ok but the people just walk on, in their own peculiar night dance, the rhythms of nowhere tapping out their beat through the sound of shoes on the street. I think I am going to get sick …

My   Journey

Begins

At   Its   Ending

38

Moments collide like their own pain

The swirling mass of our lives moves through the distance of our being, we

Search the universe for answers and move through the underground stations of our imagination, we

See everything and nothing at the same time, the Vortex moves to consume us, we

Move through the moments when the oracle calls to us and asks us what we want to be, we

Move across the distances that come between us and reach out our hands,

Holding hands we swim through the quantum dances of our reality, we

Are random, a collection of possibilities that calls through the Tiny motions we make with our fingers, we

Are the forming of that Sense that calls us to paint the picture of our beginning, we

Create our portrait and throw it into the

Starry heavens that surround us with their hope,

I am a million different people from this day to the next, I

Search for my existence through the trash cans and the places

that nobody goes, I

Find the cigarette butt of my old ways and throw it into the

river, imagining it sailing towards the sea like its own tiny

memory, I

Move through each time frame, a lost particle seeking its

resolution in light, I

Move to-and-fro through the phantoms of my dreaming, I

Learn to exist through refuting existence.

39

I wake up cold and uncomfortable. My whole body seems to be aching. I check my pockets and find that I have about a tenner, enough for a cheap vodka and a blanket or two from a charity shop. I stretch my arms and try and figure out what happened. I feel a bit hazy. I remember the meeting, the off license, walking. I am not sure where I am so I look for a street name. It appears that I am near Euston station.

I manage to get three blankets from the charity shop. I also note that I have a few cigarette butts in my pocket and light one of them up, breathing deeply. I cough. I can't seem to shake the feeling of being cold. I wrap the blankets around me and put an old McDonald's cup in front of me, hoping that someone will put something in it which would allow me to buy some more drink.

The day is slow. I watch the commuters walking by, clutching their *Financial Times* and moving in their own beat. I feel disconnected, as though I exist in a universe far from my own. A lady drops a coin in my cup. I smile and say, *Thank you*. I kinda wish that she would stop for a conversation, but she has her own life, her own things to do. The cold abates a bit, the blankets are quite warm. A businessman drops another coin in my cup. I smile and say, *Thank you*.

To relieve the boredom, I imagine the lives of the people with me on the street. The guy in the striped suit is definitely a banker, or possibly a stockbroker. The woman in the high-heeled shoes is the secretary for some big brokerage firm. Her boss is a bastard, but apart from that she quite likes her job. The young man with thick glasses is a student, possibly studying sciences at Imperial College. The young girl in fashionable clothes is also a student, she is studying English at University College London. The young man with the portfolio is a fine arts student, probably studying at Goldsmiths. The old man used to work in publishing but retired two years ago. The old woman is a housewife. The woman with the dog is currently unemployed, but has applied for some jobs in marketing. The man with the loud tie is a professor, maybe of anthropology ... We all have our own stories. And we make sense of our stories through the stories of others. We may sometimes seem to be separate, but we are all connected in a way. We search for the same things, a home where we can sleep in the warmth, enough money for a car, maybe a yearly sunshine break. Loving and being loved. We exist through the constructions of our lives, dancing on the thin edge between security and precariousness. I remember reading of a consultant gynaecologist in Dublin. The world was his oyster. Then he hit someone with a car who subsequently became disabled. The doctor was over the limit. The doctor was imprisoned for two and a half years and struck off the medical register. His wife began having affairs. He had no way of paying off his mortgage ...

We are all fragile. The banker, or maybe stockbroker, looks pretty sorted. But maybe he is in the middle of an acrimonious divorce. Or maybe he will be laid off in a week. It is impossible to know. Only that we are all part of this universe together and we are all trying to make sense of it. I draw on my butt and close my eyes for a second ... I decide to do an inventory of the most generous people. Those that look creative are often comparatively generous. As are some of the businessmen. Businesswomen tend to be the least generous ...

When I have collected enough money, I go to a nearby off license for some cheap vodka. I do not have enough money for the pub, and due to the state of me they would probably throw me out anyway. There is a young girl at the till and I smile and say, *Hello*. She looks severe, a slash of red lipstick and penetrating eyes. But she gives me the drink. I feel like asking her name, simply to make some sort of connection with another human being, but decide against it. She does not look particularly interested in having a conversation with me. I try to imagine her life, working in the shop all day. I feel a kind of respect for her. I wonder if anyone called the ambulance for the Pakistani shop owner. I wonder if he is ok. I take the drink and say *Thank you, have a nice week.*

The severe look melts a little. There is even the hint of a smile, *Thank you, you too.*

The   Sense

Of   Being

Hovers

Like   The   Mist

Around   The   Streetlamps

40

And so life goes on. The people moving through their own particular segments of spacetime, their lives, their routines. And my life, I take a swig from a bottle of cheap vodka and move slowly through the dreams I once had … Mary, her hair shining in the sun, her face, laughing, so alive. I am only semi-alive these days. I move through my day in a clockwork ritual that beats its own time upon the fabric of my being. I move to try and concentrate, on something, anything, but there is nothing there. Just the blank walls, the cold, a butt-end, and the vodka. I pass time in the millennia that are somehow trapped in the drink. Easing myself through … I hear the echo of Mary's voice, of the rustling trees, giving testament to our freedom. But I am not there, I will never be able to go back there. All that exists are the nameless faces passing me on the street who occasionally place a few coins in my cup. Who clutch their *Financial Times* like identity. I am trying to figure out my reality, what it all means, how we exist. I focus on one of the pedestrians. He is young, about my age, and is smartly dressed. He is about my age but the distance is immense. I try to enter his world a little bit, going to the office, drinking polystyrene coffee, making deals on the telephone. Maybe he has a girlfriend. Maybe they hope to get a mortgage together. I suddenly feel the weight of my disconnect, the sense that the world and I are on different trajectories and will never intersect. I imagine society and I to be on parallel lines, stretching into the infinity of our particular histories but never meeting ... A woman places a coin in my cup and I say, *Thank you*. Another tiny moment in the fabric of life, a brief glimpse of ... what? How much one needs to connect. I move through a universe that I defined myself, ages ago, I drift through it holding my head. It seems that the world is spinning out of control. I realize that I need some of Nick's blue pills but I appear to have lost his telephone number ... My mind begins to ache. I feel a pain that seems to spread through my head and from there to every bone in my body. I feel I am going to get sick, but I hold it back. Everything seems to be going fast, too fast. I pull the blankets around myself to find a little warmth. I find my whole body to be shaking, this awful cold. I take another drink but that makes me feel worse. I find a cigarette butt and smoke it frantically, controlled breathing, in, out, in, out, try to relax, in, out, in, out, I need to relax ... The people on the street merge into a homogeneous mass. They flow into each other, drifting through their awareness as one body containing a million bodies, each one shouting silently the pain that I feel inside me, calling through the mountaintops of forgetting, getting lost in the street lamps whose light appears to devour them ... breathe, in, out, in, out ... moving through little motions with my fingers, feeling a spark of light that shoots off one of the street lamps and ends up in my hand, so tiny, so delicate ... And then the light grows. It becomes a star, and then a supernova, exploding in my hands and taking me with it across the universe and into the empty blackness of deep space, breathe, in, out, in, out ... My head feels disconnected, moving above my body. I look down on myself, the figure huddled under the blankets clutching the bottle of vodka like it is the only thing left in the entire universe. I feel like screaming and I open my mouth but no sound comes. I think of the fact of one particle being able to communicate instantaneously with another in a process called quantum entanglement. My mind is communicating instantaneously with my body but they don't connect. They drift apart, still communicating, but the distance grows huge. I feel sick but I can't vomit. I move through this awful pain, the night crystallizing through the street lamps and the sensation of being tired, so tired. Moving through the spaces that exist between the different parts of me, ever communicating but ever separate ...

Life

Collapses

Within

The   Swansong

Of   My   Being

41

Distances move within one another,
The starlight scatters us in the form of its singing
I find, a thousand years ago, some distant call to the
Memories that call me through the cliff face of their reality
Moving through the call of the bird as it finds its freedom
through the glistening clouds of our summer
I will always remember the laughter and the holding of hands
I will always remember those stolen moments that I hold
against my heart as an antidote to the pain
Like the healing blanket of ages, you wrap yourself around me
and keep me warm
But now there is only the distance, the silent tears that spatter
on the floor of our history
What was has become a ghost
The desert sand fills the cup of my loneliness as I drink to
memory and forgetting
The sand swirls around me like the dance of its own phantom

More beautiful than the rose, I catch you in my mind

I breathe with you as we levitate through the shimmer of our dreams

You are the only reality in this unreal world

You are the song through which my life gave birth to itself

You are the bird call in the forest seeking to celebrate its meaning

I saw you a million miles away when the star gave birth to itself

I saw you twirling, drops of Jupiter in your hair,

And now the empty box of memories stolen by Fate

The call that no one answers has some sprite of thought that evaporates as soon as it is born

Hold my hand again, in my memory at least

Laugh with me again, in my memory at least

Breathe the warmth that exists through our endless dance together

Show yourself in the neon, show yourself once more before I fall into this restless sleep of nothingness.

42

The night stretches itself out before me. My head is spinning faster now, I grip onto my legs and rock to-and-fro, to-and-fro. The images of a million imaginations freeze around the street lamps, moving through the moments that they were born in, moving in a kaleidoscope of nightmare that sings its panic through my aching head. I feel that I don't exist, that I am some sort of virtual reality being dreamt of by a games programmer while he was high on acid. The panic rises to a crescendo, moving through the street lamps. There is the normal array of night people, people selling drugs, prostitutes. I move within all of them and yet ultimately separate, always separate … My hands begin to shake uncontrollably, and the cold … it cuts through the very fabric of me. I draw the blankets closer and sing a song to myself, *Jingle Bells* I don't know why that particular song, maybe some distant call from a childhood that evaporated long ago. *Jingle Bells, Jingle Bells, Jingle all the Way* … I clutch my head with my hands *Oh what fun it is to ride. In a one-horse open sleigh* … I begin to cough uncontrollably, a hacking cough, I need a cigarette.

Thankfully I find a butt in one of my pockets. I light it and smoke compulsively with my hands shaking. I remember when I last saw Mary, her hands quivering all the time and the single, silent tear down the side of her face ... Mary seems to call out, *John!* but I am unable to answer. I reach out to touch her but she is gone, fading with the night that casts its one final songline to the altar of the street lamps, a sacrifice to the realities that evaporate across the seas of our being ...

Distance   Finds

Its   Own   Direction

Through

The   Riemann   Sphere

Of   Our   Lives

43

I hear the noise of some people coming towards me. They are obviously drunk, high, or both. They weave around the street, shouting. One of them seems to say *Look at that guy. Shall we give him a fright?* He is apparently referring to me. I begin to feel nervous. I have connected a little bit more with the reality around me but my head is still spinning. I continue to sing *Jingle Bells, Jingle Bells, Jingle all the way …* The lads move closer until they are virtually on top of me. I feel panic rising up like a volcano, spewing lava, growing, becoming, consuming … I remember the knife that Mike gave me when we went to thrash the Asian store. I clutch onto it like redemption. The youths get closer and I clutch the knife hard, hiding it under my blankets but gripping … My head still seems to float above my body. I move slowly underneath the blankets and try and control my breathing again. I try to concentrate on everything, my head, the youths, the knife, the form of a desire to be anywhere but here gripping my mind like paralysis …

One of the youths leans over me. I go into automaton mode, reflexes, that is all. No thought. No consideration. Just react. React simply. Simply react. I take the knife and lash out at the youth. I think I cut his face. There is blood and a lot of shouting. One of the youths calls out *Help! He has a knife! He stabbed Martin!* Martin, I guess that is his name, grips his face and starts crying. The blood drips onto his hands and he is shaking, kind of like the way I was shaking a while back. For the first time in what seems to be days, I feel a sense of clarity. My entirety is focused on this moment, this moment is the entirety of my existence, *I am.* I am because everything has crystalized on this particular location in spacetime. The universe revolves around this particular moment. The dreams evaporate and all that is left is here, now … I sway to-and-fro, *Jingle bells, Jingle Bells, Jingle all the way* … Nothing exists. I exist. I am the testament to existence's nothingness. I dance with Shiva, god of life, god of death. I say a silent prayer to the bottle of vodka beside me, to the roll-up that sticks to my lips as if reciting its own story … The youths have gone, some smattering of blood on the street the only memory I have of them like some sort of signature tune that wrote its reality and surreality on the pavement, casting its identity for all to see, *this is …*

The   Direction

Of   Our   Songline

That   Defines

The   Multiple   Legends

Through   Which

We   Are   Named

44

I notice the youths returning, accompanied by the police. The youth I think is called Martin describes me attacking him with the knife, *I was just going to put some money in his cup and he went for me.* The police then ask me what happened. I sit, silently singing, *Jingle Bells, Jingle Bells, Jingle all the way* ... my motionlessness intersecting with the moment. I find myself in some coordinate I cannot define, through some geometry that makes no sense to me. I imagine floating like a satellite, beaming down my information to Planet Earth below ... *This is me. This is who I am. Recognize me. It is the only way that I can recognize myself.* The policeman continues to ask me what happened, *You have the right to remain silent* ... I focus on the policeman's shoes, imagining him walking and walking, walking through the jungle, and the desert, and London, each step a search for control that shimmers but is ultimately ephemeral. I sit in silence, just focusing. The youths are shouting and one of the policemen takes notes. I squeeze myself through my dreaming and try again to breathe. I feel suffocated, like someone is strangling me. My breath becomes slower and slower. I feel tired again, so tired. I lean my head against the shop window where I am sitting and wrap the blanket around me. *I feel nothing. I am comfortably numb. The numbness is the only reality that my existence has.* I close my eyes and drift off ...

Silence

Creates

Its   Own   Image

Through

The   Calm   Blue   Water

Between   Us

45

I find myself in a small room with nicotine-stained walls and an ashtray. My head hurts. I long for a coffee, or something, something warm. I stretch my arms above my head and try to make sense of my environment. A man comes in holding a polystyrene coffee and a pack of cigarettes. He gives me the coffee and offers me a smoke which I accept gratefully.

What is your name?

John.

Do you know why you are here?

Not really.

Do you remember anything about last night?

Not really.

You injured someone, quite badly.

I'm sorry ... my head is hurting.

They are pressing charges.

My head is hurting …

I focus on a piece of chewing gum stuck to the wall. *Focus. Concentrate. Exist. Be. I am …* The chewing gum seems like a summary of everything, stuck against the wall against its will, calling to some alternate reality … my head is spinning, *concentrate, focus …* I move in my seat a little. My legs are aching and I feel the need to stretch them out. I feel uncomfortable, watched, like some zoo curiosity whose only meaning in life is to entertain the tourists … I breathe inside of myself, I put my hands to my eyes … *I have seen too much* … I wrap my hands around the polystyrene coffee, enjoying its warmth … I am still shivering *that blasted cold …* I take a sip and the watery liquid eases something, I begin to wake up a little bit, and move towards trying to make sense of my surroundings which seem kinda summarized by the chewing gum. I get up and walk around a little.

The man comes in, *Did you enjoy your coffee?*

Yes.

Would you like another one?

Yes please.

And another cigarette?

Yes please.

My responses seem automatic. It is not me responding but some avatar pretending to be me. We are all caught in this computer game, we are all just a simulation. The man with the coffee is a simulation, invented by some alien being who enjoys computer games. I am a simulation. Each movement preordained. My fate and the fate of the world lie hand-in-hand in some swirling dance of delirium. I move slowly. It is as if my movements are controlled. Shiva has a joystick and each movement defines the pattern of his creating. Shiva drags the joystick to the left, I move my leg. He drags it to the right, I drink my polystyrene coffee. And the man with the coffee, Shiva moves the joystick to the left, and he comes to sit opposite me placing the pack of cigarettes on the table between us. Shiva moves the joystick to the right, and he takes out another cigarette and offers it to me. Shiva pulls the joystick to the left, and I have a drag.

He asks me again, *Do you remember anything about last night?*

I am in slow motion. My head is hurting.

It is important that you tell me. The person who claims that you attacked him is pressing charges ...

I state, *My head is hurting.*

164

Please try to remember.

I focus on the chewing gum. It morphs into the only thing that actually exists in the room. The man, me, we are both phantoms. And the cigarettes and the polystyrene coffee are figments of our imagination. *Concentrate. Concentrate …*

I have to, erm, concentrate.

My eyes become blurry and the chewing gum goes in and out of focus. *Concentrate, concentrate.* I take a pull of my cigarette and another sip of coffee. *Concentrate, concentrate.*

The piece of chewing gum has suddenly grown enormous. It is filling the whole room, it moves to consume me, the man, the cigarettes, the polystyrene coffee, expanding like some sort of nightmarish Golem who comes to life through the smoke of the cigarettes, the steam from the coffee … I grip the bottom of my chair and breathe hard …

I am … you know, homeless. I was asleep when the youths approached me. They were shouting and I was scared. I got into the habit of taking these pills, but I had run out. I felt awful, like my whole body was collapsing. Like my mind had left my body and was floating somewhere else. I think the youths were trying to scare me. I don't know. I lashed out, I think. I cut one of them, I think …

Where did you get the knife?

It was given to me by some guys I used to know that were into all this white supremacy shit. They wanted to scare an Asian shopkeeper and we all had knives. I didn't want any part of it, and I walked away. I had nowhere else to go. That is why I was homeless. I kind of forgot that I had the knife. But London is dangerous ...

The piece of chewing gum is breathing, growing and shrinking, growing and shrinking.

Self-control ...

I feel desperately tired. Everything aches. I ask to go to sleep. I am placed in a holding cell and fall asleep.

Fabrications

Create

Their   Own   Realities

When   Faced

With   The   Function

Of

Our   Dreaming

46

I walk through the forest. The sun shatters its light upon the leaves that flow through the wind eddy upwards, catching the light and sparkling. I reach to touch one and it floats through my hands like an ephemeral dream. I rise upwards, tickled by the leaves and I am laughing. The sunlight turns yellow, red, purple. The sky shatters in a myriad of colour and I am floating, floating through it ... I see Mary walking on the waters of the lake. Her hair gleams and the sun sings in celebration. The sky is orange, blue ... little crystals emerge and glisten, changing colour like Christmas tree lights sparkling off the light and leaves. The grass grows taller, so tall that it can reach our heads. We run through the grass holding hands ... we echo our song and then rise upwards. We float beyond the cliffs where the salt spray crashes itself against the rocks like memory. We move through the silent clouds with the salt spray taste upon our tongues. We create our existence a thousand times. And the stars glisten their memory through us all, growing and filling the night sky with their brightness, a cacophony of colour, yellow, red, purple, moving through their histories. The particle moves and collapses into a thousand other particles. Each one moves in its own dance. Each one paints itself, yellow, red, purple. Each one rises through our laughter like stardust. The wind blows through the grass and sings its own Magnificat. The songs of creation permeate everything, the fabric of how we come to be. And there is Mary, her hands outstretched, running through the grass and singing her song to it. And the leaves flicker in chorus. We move through a thousand images. A bird lands on Mary's hand and sings its song to her before rising her up into the sky where she shimmers in the light shards caught by the leaves, the image of a thousand places ... I am at school, staring out of the window when Mary flows by. I float outside of the open crack at the top of the window and dance with her. We stand underneath a tree and a thousand birds call us into their song ...

And then the sun crashes out of the sky. The birds disappear. And Mary is sucked into a vortex, becoming smaller and smaller. I reach out my hand to save her but she is gone.

And then I am at a West Ham match. 'The referee's a wanker!' And the referee floats above the stadium blowing his whistle frantically. And West Ham wins 5-0. But the match has to be replayed because of what happened to the referee.

And then I am on the streets. My blanket is the Golden Fleece from Jason and the Argonauts. It protects me. But then someone called Nick steals it, and I am left with nothing but the sense of cold, this freezing cold …

I wake up and look around me. My head still aches and I am desperate for a drink. The man from yesterday comes in with a polystyrene coffee and a pack of cigarettes. He gives me the coffee and a cigarette and asks me how I feel. *Awful. I need a drink.*

He apologizes, *We only do coffee.* He smiles a bit and I feel a kind of connection that I haven't felt for months.

I say that I was dreaming last night. I pull on my cigarette. I need a drink. *Need a drink.* The polystyrene coffee burns my throat.

I Sing

My   Reality

To   You

Through

The   Woven   Carpet

Of

My   Primal   Scream

47

The trial occurs as if a dream. I stand there as people argue, people present evidence. It is a process outside of me, a theatre in which I am neither the performer nor the audience, some distant formation through which each person seems to float and the judge seems to transfigure and become an enormous giant who grows and fills the entire room like the chewing gum in the police station. For myself, I don't care too much about the result. My life has undergone gravitational collapse anyway and the verdict doesn't matter. Just another game in the eternal computer game of life. Shiva presses the 'enter' key and the judge's mouth opens and shuts like a fish. Shiva presses the 'A' key and the lawyers move sideways, and sideways. I entertain myself through the process of imagining this. One of the lawyers calls the youth, Martin, to the witness box. He describes that I viciously attacked him when he tried to put some money in the McDonald's cup. That is not how I remember it. But I was kinda hazy at the time. I look at the light above the judge's head and feel that I am floating into it, that I am back at school, that I am in trouble again for disturbing the class. The judge turns into the headmaster, *This is not good enough. We have to do something about your behaviour.* I remember the school food, the rugby, the slow strangling of any process that might be deemed creative. I remember all those who believed that I had disappointed them, teachers, parents. I wonder if I have disappointed the man with the polystyrene coffee in some way. I remember the crack of the teacher's ruler upon my hand, *one is here to be punished.* Life is a dance between crime and punishment. Life seems like a process of doing something wrong. I remember reading Kafka, about a man who stood trial but neither the judges nor himself knew what for. Life is a trial. We are examined and re-examined. We move through the rite of being corrected, every stage of life is met through correction ... The judge sits ever so still like a fossil dug up by some archaeologist as a relic from a past where things existed differently, where dinosaurs roamed. I imagine my schoolteachers as dinosaurs, stomping around in their awkwardness, teeth bared, snarling at the world, seeking their prey. And their prey is our imaginations, they crunch them up until there is nothing left of us. And when one tries to be oneself in any way the jaws open, and the teacher-cum-dinosaur swallows you up. All of you. Because you did not like sport. Because you found Irish grammar boring. And there they are, lurking in their war against intelligence, striving to create a being that they can define as normal, as acceptable. Correction is the ultimate rite of passage. And when one has been punished for one thing, one moves through to being punished for something else. And life is a routine of slaps, report cards, being brought before the headmaster ... *the slap of the ruler on the wrist* ... because that is how we come to be defined, this is the oracle of our worth.

I come to understand that I have been handed down a prison sentence of one year. The moment freezes me in a type of singularity, I am not sure whether I am frightened or silently relieved. Prison is somewhere to go. Prison is real. One does one's time. That is real. One is given a number, and one exists. There is a record of you, therefore you are. I am no' 777. So that is me. We dispense with names and get to something real. And we become. We become ourselves through being distilled into a moment, distilled into a way of being, distilled like Scottish Malt Whiskey, purer and purer until absolute purity is met. And we taste this purity like redemption *Silent Night, Silent Night. All is Calm, All is Bright* ...

We   Move   Through

Our   Own

Particular

Spacetime

Coordinates

In   The   Journey

Towards

Our   Ultimate   Self-discovery

48

As we enter the prison, the other prisoners gather round. They appear to be taking bets as to which one of us new guys will collapse first. I hear one lad, an Afro-Caribbean lad, bet 10 cigarettes on, *The skinny guy over there with the posh accent.* I take this to mean myself.

We are given our clothes, and a Bible, and shown to our cells. There is a lot of noise. The prisoners who had laid bets on which one of us new guys would break down first were busily trying to goad their 'horses'. Cigarettes are a powerful currency in prison. Eventually a seemingly shy, plump guy starts crying. Those of the older prisoners who had bet on him begin to celebrate. I wonder what his name is.

Prison is about routine. You eat when they say you eat. You eat what they say you eat. You go to the toilet when they say that you go to the toilet.

I keep myself to myself for a while. I begin reading compulsively. Books pass the time. And they are a way of getting a bit of stimulation. I don't know if the others find me a bit stand-offish. I don't mean to be. But solitude calls to me. It gives me a chance to think, to work things out. And I can just close my eyes and dream, dream I am somewhere else, a youth again, with Mary …

About two weeks in, the young Afro-Caribbean lad comes to join me. *You cost me 10 smokes.* His face is smiling. There is no aggression. *What are you in for?*

Grievous Bodily Harm, and you?

Breaking and entering. What's your name?

John, and yours?

Steve. Steve looks at a West Ham tattoo I had done. *Are you into all that football hooliganism white supremacy shit?*

I reply, *Sort of, for a while. I didn't really believe in it but it gave me an excuse to be angry, to hate. I needed an excuse to hate.* I tell him about Mary and he seems sympathetic. He also offers to get me stuff like smokes, or a bit of ganja if that is my thing. I thank him very much.

We begin to sit together a lot. He tells me of his own life, that he was brought up in Brixton and that his family was poor. His father drank (I say that so did mine) and used to hit the kids a bit. He got into trouble at school for using drugs and

177

was expelled. There weren't exactly many job opportunities so he took to stealing stuff.

At first it was just bicycles and shit but I got involved with a group who were more ambitious. We started breaking into houses. Jewellery was what we were mainly after, but also things like televisions, microwaves ... We broke into this house in Hamstead. A real nice house. Then the owner came back. One of us panicked and hit him. He was injured but otherwise ok. Then the police came. They told me to drop the television. I said that if I dropped the television it would break and that I would have to face charges of destruction of property too ... He smiled broadly.

I begin to laugh.

The   Mystery

Of   Redemption

Is   Its   Choice

Of   The   Unexpected

49

And time goes on. I get a calendar and mark each day. When I first get here I have problems withdrawing from the drink and the blue pills, but after a couple of weeks I feel clearer. The place has a strange sense of security. Steve and I always sit together at mealtimes and he begins to introduce me to some of the others. Rodney used to sell televisions. Pete is in for armed robberies. He also tells me the ones to avoid. *There are some people here who are real mean. Watch your back a little bit.* He points to a rough-looking man with blond hair. I begin to fit in a little and the time becomes tolerable. There are some things on the outside that I miss, but the best in my life has been taken so there is little to mourn. I enjoy the chance to read. Visiting times are lonely for me. No one comes. But beyond that I form a kind of acceptance. One can hide behind the routine. The routine is good at masking stuff. And I have, with Steve and his friends, the connection I have longed for. We trade in cigarettes, vital currency, and sit and play checkers and backgammon. We play backgammon gambling style, using the cigarettes as chips. I become good at it and always have plenty of smokes which I can trade for stuff like posters, or my own books. I ask Steve whether he misses the outside. He says that he misses his mates and his sister, he adores his sister, but otherwise not really. Life has not been particularly kind to him either. His sister comes every visiting time to see him and brings large numbers of cigarettes for him to trade. *That's what I look forward most to when I leave here, being with my sister. She was always there when father hit me, she always tried to calm him down ...*

Images

Flow

In   A   Thousand

Directions

Before

They   Find

A   Place

To   Rest

50

So, I write everything down. I sit with Steve at mealtimes and we discuss our lives. So different yet in a way so similar, the feeling of disconnect. I exist through the routine of things, moving through to each repetition in search of a reason, any reason. I lie in my bed at night and dream of Mary, West Ham, everything, seeking the sort of enlightenment that shimmers like the moonlight on the lake. Searching for something, I don't yet know what, but maybe it will become clearer as I write it all down. Doing time is slow, but one finds a strange comfort in the predictability of things … maybe the predictability is the ultimate enlightenment. We concentrate on the simple process of living. All other complications are simply washed away. Every day of time I do, I mark it off on my calendar, coming closer to release which I long for and dread at the same time. Sometimes I feel like I am floating above myself, looking down on my body and mind as I enter into some kind of hallucinogenic dream-time through which my life replays itself, over and over, seeking meaning in the endless repetitions and the processes through which we live here. My existence is caught up in a thread that winds itself over itself in never-ending repetitions of the thoughts and doubts that have stalked me since childhood. I think of the Asian shop owner and wonder if he is ok. I think of the cacophony of aggression that was part of my London life. And I think of Mary, laughing against the sun and sparkling in her radiance ... elements that flow through my awareness, that weave through my imagination, semi-ghosts calling me to my abstractions, the abstractions of the world, both ... I imagine Mary and I to be entangled particles, destined to connect whatever the space between us. I think of how distant I have become from the ways of my upbringing and hold on to this thought as a comfort ... one can always escape. Maybe you have to be imprisoned to be truly free. Here the outside world does not touch you. All that exists is the daily routine. We escape from the outside as if through some kind of religion that offers the freedom to disconnect. With everything. With all the pain and all the confusion. The routine becomes addictive, I long for it like some kind of junkie whose life is determined by his next fix. I find myself in a kind of monastery existence through which everything is reduced to its ultimate state, moments condensed through mealtimes and exercise. I get contraband cigarettes from Steve and smoke them, finding release that comes through the process of breathing and doing nothing more, inhaling the smoke like redemption. I think of my parents, the silence that shrieked like a banshee across the dining table as we ate. I think of all the things that were, and all the things that could have been. We make choices. It is part of life's process. And I think of the choices I have made, both good and bad. I think of Mary, her red hair glinting in the sun. I think of beating the crap out of someone because he supported the wrong football team. Or because he was Asian. We seek the meaning behind the processes that have defined our lives. In one's dreams one can become anything, one simply moves through one's imagination ... I lie on my bed and imagine that I am a politician with the power to determine the fates of others. Ultimately, I wish to determine my own fate. One finds that when everything has been taken from you, you are at your most free. Because there are no ties, no obligations, one becomes distilled in an abstraction that through its ultimate simplicity insulates one from all the pain. ... I psychologically wrap it around myself like the blankets I used to wrap around myself to ward off the cold when I was homeless. The abstraction calls like a Zen kōan that calls us to relinquish the fact of our lives and to enter into some kind of crystalline spiritus that drifts through its own meaning by refuting the meaning of the world. Baked beans on toast, again. We reduce, and find ourselves expanding through that reduction. One becomes the ultimate 'I' stripped of everything but the pure essence of ourselves … I can be whatever I want to be. I imagine giving a speech at Speakers' Corner, calling all others to relinquish that which I myself am trying to relinquish. They say in Islam that the greatest jihad of all is the jihad within. And I form of my own personal jihad through the beans on toast and the dreaming that comes with lights out. I can be whatever I want to be because I have learned to be nothing at all …

Distance

Moves

Itself

As   The   Ultimate

Connection

Between   Us

AFTERWORD 1

The time of my release. I have a small bag with my scant belongings and I walk through the gates looking round me like I have landed on a strange and unfamiliar planet where I don't speak the language. It is a bright, sunny day and I feel the warmth on my back as I walk. The leaves glisten green almost like hallucinations and a gentle wind blows against me. I had never realized how truly beautiful the world is ... when one has been stripped of everything even the shimmer of a leaf is some form of miracle ...

I find a small bedsit and contact a group called NACRO who specialize in the rehabilitation of persons who have been in prison. I meet with the director and get placed on a carpentry course. There are about 10 others and we seem to almost instantly strike a rapport. I make a particular friend with a man called Bill who was in prison for smashing the window of a jewellery store and trying to steal its contents. Bill is an ex-junkie and explains that the only way to get his next fix was to rob stuff. But he is hoping to start again with a bone fide career. We often go for a drink afterwards, and exchange memories ... life is about connection ...

On qualification, I get a bit of work on the building sites. I don't earn an absolute fortune, but I can live comfortably. I sometimes go to the prison to visit Steve, bringing some boxes of cigarettes with me that he can either smoke himself or sell as contraband. I have discovered that the barriers between us are only figments of our own construction. I never had much problem with my posh-ish accent through my time in prison unlike at school where I was teased constantly. We live in a connected universe and it is made real through these connections. Each one of us trying to find meaning through the meanings of others. We create the paths that we walk along from the paths given to us by others. We exist as a common humanity, in all the loves gained and lost, in all the jihads that we fight within ourselves in our search to find a life that is liveable. We exist to dance with the universe in all its creativity and vibrancy and to find that song that begins with each morning as the birds fly over the lake ...

The   Images   That   We   Find

Form   The   Fabric

Of   The   Music

Of   Our   Dreaming

AFTERWORD 2

The shimmer of our freedom catches itself through the
Breathing-in of a gentle day that calls us to
Spin with its creativity, rising up and not looking downwards, I
Move through the song through which I came to
Translate a thousand images that call to me across the
slipstream, I
Enter the universal tune and spiral upward with the songbirds
that
Make their music on the interface of our being like some
Opera of existence, the music rising up so as to glorify the
Gods of our imagination.

AFTERWORD 3

I decide to try and find Finn. I manage to get his details through Barnardos and, with some trepidation call his new parents. A lady called Ann answers the phone. She seems kind and gentle. I explain who I am and ask her whether I can see Finn. She agrees.

I get on an Aer Lingus flight from Heathrow to Cork. It seems strange to see Ireland again, the memories, the joy, the pain. It is a nice day on landing. I book myself into a small Bed & Breakfast in Cork city and arrange to meet Finn the next day. I decide to take him to Fota Wildlife Park.

We catch the train from Cork city to Fota, not talking much. I guess we are both a bit shy of each other. But when we reach the wildlife park we open up a bit. Finn is particularly taken with the lemurs. He also loves the cheetahs. We are lucky because the cheetahs are being fed. This seems to fascinate Finn, he points to them, smiling and laughing.

We decide to stop for an ice cream and Finn looks at me,

What was mammy like?

I reply, *The most beautiful woman in the world.*

Tiny

Moments

Of   Happiness

Caught

In   The   Holding

Of   Hands

AFTERWORD 4

Those driftwood memories through which we seek ourselves
Flow through the slipstream of our lives and
Motion to us through, the
Tiny movements through which the dance begins
Moving within and without ourselves, we
Catch our dreams on the edge of a knife and
Spin with the pain and the ecstasy through which we are born
and then die in, the
Transformation of autumn into winter and then into spring
again, we
Move through the leaf-rustle moments through which our
Meanings whisper themselves into being only to fade into the
skies of our evening, we
Are and we are not, imagining that probability moment in
which, we
Play games with fate and learn of its laughter and its crying, the
Tears of a thousand ages cascade upon the rocks by the water,

in which, we

Dabbled our feet, and flickered like the fishes, I

Saw you in a thousand dreams and caught you in a thousand
songs, I

Raised you in the spirit of your celebration, I

Moved through the being of you, beckoning you to

Take my hand and spin through the moment of our creation, the

Driftwood memories we hold explain and deny our existence, we

Move through them so as to weave a fabric of ourselves to

Throw upon the water and watch float in the dance of our

imaginations caught Spinning in the Silent theatre of our lives.

Mel O'Dea is an artist, writer and poet. She has exhibited in London and Ireland, and as a writer has had two books published and contributed to various magazines. She is an advocate of human rights and has campaigned for the Anti-Apartheid Movement since her student days at Durham University in the late 1980s. Having had an eclectic education in both the arts and sciences, her initial career was in microelectronics. Mel now lives in Mallow, Co Cork, Ireland, and shares her accommodation with a small black and white Friend called Rainbow Dog.

Novels by the same Author:

The Ghost Whisperers

Figments

The Silken Thread

(upcoming at time of publication)